Massachusetts MCAS Grade 6 Math Workbook

Practice Problems & Exercises with Answer Key

Dr. A. Nazari

Published by View Math Education

ViewMath.com

YOUR MATH PRACTICE STARTS HERE

Grade 6 Math Workbook

Practice Problems • Word Problems • Complete Answer Key

Math gets stronger with practice — and this workbook gives you plenty of it. Every section starts with a quick reminder of the key concept, then moves straight into problems that go from comfortable to challenging.

Work at your own pace. Show your steps on scratch paper. Then use the answer key in the back to check your work, spot mistakes, and learn from them. That's how real progress happens.

44 Topics Across 5 Chapters

From ratios and percents to equations, geometry, and statistics — every Grade 6 standard is covered.

Progressive Difficulty

Each topic builds from basic recall to multi-step problems, so you grow your confidence as you go.

Real-World Word Problems

Apply what you learn to everyday situations — shopping, cooking, building, sports, and more.

Complete Answer Key

Every problem has an answer in the back. Check your work, find your mistakes, and try again.

How to Use This Workbook

Four simple steps to get the most out of every section.

1

Read the Quick Review

Each section opens with a short summary of the key formula or concept. If anything feels unfamiliar, pair this workbook with the study guide for a deeper explanation before jumping into problems.

2

Work the Problems in Order

Problems are arranged from basic to challenging. Starting with the easier ones builds confidence and warms up your thinking before the harder questions arrive.

3

Show Your Work

Write out every step on scratch paper. If you get a wrong answer, your written work will help you pinpoint exactly where things went off track — so you can fix it and learn.

4

Check Answers and Learn

After finishing a section, flip to the Answer Key and check every problem. For each mistake, figure out why it happened, then try a similar problem again.

Suggested Weekly Routine

- ***Monday–Thursday:*** *Complete one topic per day (about 20–30 minutes).*
- ***Friday:*** *Review mistakes from the week and re-do any problem you missed.*
- ***Weekend:*** *Take a break — or try a challenge problem for fun!*

Pair It Up

This workbook focuses on practice. For full explanations, worked examples, and teaching notes, use it alongside the Grade 6 Study Guide or a classroom textbook.

What's Inside This Workbook

Every topic you'll practice, chapter by chapter.

Chapter 1: Ratios, Rates, and Percents

10 topics

- *What Is a Ratio?*
- *Using Ratio Language*
- *What Is a Rate?*
- *Finding the Unit Rate*
- *Tables of Equivalent Ratios*
- *Graphing Ratios*
- *What Is a Percent?*
- *Solving Percent Problems*
- *Rate & Ratio Word Problems*
- *Converting Measurement Units*

Chapter 2: The Number System

11 topics

- *Dividing Fractions by Fractions*
- *Multi-Digit Division*
- *Decimal Operations*
- *GCF and LCM*
- *Distributive Property*
- *Positive & Negative Numbers*
- *Opposites and Absolute Value*
- *Rational Numbers on the Line*
- *The Coordinate Plane*
- *Comparing Rational Numbers*
- *Distance on the Coord. Plane*

Chapter 3: Expressions and Equations

10 topics

- *Exponents & Order of Operations*
- *Words into Expressions*
- *Terms, Factors, Coefficients*
- *Evaluating Expressions*
- *Equivalent Expressions*
- *Variables in Real-World Problems*
- *Solving One-Step Equations*
- *Writing Inequalities*
- *Graphing Inequalities*
- *Two Quantities That Change*

Chapter 4: Geometry — Area, Surface Area, and Volume 6 topics

- Area of Triangles
- Area of Parallelograms & Trapezoids
- Volume of Rectangular Prisms
- Polygons on the Coordinate Plane
- Finding Area on the Coord. Plane
- Nets and Surface Area

Chapter 5: Statistics and Data 7 topics

- Statistical Questions
- Describing Data: Center, Spread, Shape
- Mean and Median
- Measures of Spread
- Dot Plots and Histograms
- Box Plots
- Summarizing Data & Comparisons

44 topics • 5 chapters • Complete answer key included

What You'll Need

Gather these supplies before you start.

Essentials

- ☑ ***Pencils*** — *at least two sharpened pencils.*
- ☑ ***Eraser*** — *mistakes are part of learning.*
- ☑ ***Scratch paper*** — *for showing your work.*
- ☑ ***Ruler*** — *for geometry and number lines.*

Helpful Extras

- ☑ ***Colored pencils*** — *for graphs, diagrams, and the coordinate plane.*
- ☑ ***Calculator*** — *check your arithmetic after solving by hand.*
- ☑ ***Highlighter*** — *mark key formulas and vocabulary.*
- ☑ ***Notebook*** — *keep your work organized in one place.*

Study Space Tips

- *Find a quiet spot with good light.*
- *Put your phone out of reach.*
- *Set a timer for 20–30 minutes, then take a short break.*
- *Keep a water bottle nearby.*

You don't need everything at once. Pencil, eraser, and this book are enough to get started.

Formula Reference Sheet

Area Formulas

Rectangle $A = l \times w$

Parallelogram $A = b \times h$

Triangle $A = \frac{1}{2} \times b \times h$

Trapezoid $A = \frac{1}{2}(b_1 + b_2) \times h$

Volume

Rectangular Prism $V = l \times w \times h$

Surface Area

Find the area of each face, then add them all up.

Rectangular Prism:

SA $= 2lw + 2lh + 2wh$

Order of Operations

P *Parentheses first*

E *Exponents*

M/D *Multiply & Divide (left to right)*

A/S *Add & Subtract (left to right)*

Ratios & Percents

Ratio: $a : b$ *or* $\frac{a}{b}$

Unit rate: *amount per 1 unit*

Percent: *a ratio out of 100*

Part $=$ *Percent* $\times$ *Whole*

Integers & Absolute Value

Integers:

$\ldots, -3, -2, -1, 0, 1, 2, 3, \ldots$

$|-5| = 5 \quad |5| = 5$

Absolute value = distance from 0

Expressions & Equations

Exponent: $3^4 = 3 \times 3 \times 3 \times 3 = 81$

Variable: *a letter that stands for a number*

Equation: *two expressions joined by* $=$

Inequality: *uses* $<$, $>$, $\leq$, $\geq$

Coordinate Plane

Ordered pair: (x, y)

x*-axis: horizontal* y*-axis: vertical*

Origin: $(0, 0)$

Four quadrants (I, II, III, IV)

Statistics

Mean: *sum of values* $\div$ *count*

Median: *middle value (sorted)*

Range: *max − min*

Key Math Vocabulary

Words you'll see again and again in Grade 6 math.

Ratios & Rates

Ratio — A comparison of two quantities.

Equivalent ratios — Ratios that represent the same relationship.

Rate — A ratio comparing two different units.

Unit rate — A rate with a denominator of 1.

Percent — A ratio that compares a number to 100.

The Number System

Integer — A whole number or its opposite ($\ldots -2, -1, 0, 1, 2 \ldots$).

Rational number — Any number that can be written as a fraction.

Absolute value — The distance of a number from zero on a number line.

Opposite — Two numbers the same distance from zero on opposite sides.

Reciprocal — Flip the numerator and denominator: the reciprocal of $\frac{2}{3}$ is $\frac{3}{2}$.

GCF — Greatest Common Factor — the largest factor shared by two numbers.

LCM — Least Common Multiple — the smallest multiple shared by two numbers.

Expressions & Equations

Variable — A letter that represents an unknown number.

Coefficient — The number multiplied by a variable (6 in $6x$).

Constant — A fixed number with no variable ($+3$ in $2x+3$).

Expression — Numbers, variables, and operations combined (no $=$ sign).

Equation — A statement that two expressions are equal.

Inequality — A statement that uses $<, >, \leq$, or $\geq$.

Exponent — Tells how many times to multiply a base by itself.

Distributive property — $a(b+c) = ab + ac$.

Geometry

Area — The space inside a flat shape, in square units.

Base — The bottom side of a shape (or any side used for the formula).

Height — The perpendicular distance from the base to the top.

Volume — The space inside a 3-D shape, in cubic units.

Surface area — The total area of all faces of a 3-D shape.

Net — A flat pattern that folds into a 3-D shape.

Face — A flat surface of a solid figure.

Edge — The line segment where two faces meet.

Vertex — A point where edges meet.

Coordinate Plane

Ordered pair — *A pair* (x, y) *that names a location on the plane.*

Origin — *The point* $(0, 0)$ *where the axes cross.*

Quadrant — *One of the four sections of the coordinate plane.*

x***-axis*** — *The horizontal number line.*

y***-axis*** — *The vertical number line.*

Statistics & Data

Mean — *The average — sum of values divided by the count.*

Median — *The middle value when data is in order.*

Range — *The difference between the greatest and least values.*

Dot plot — *A number line with dots showing data frequency.*

Histogram — *A bar graph that shows data grouped in intervals.*

Box plot — *A diagram showing the five-number summary of data.*

IQR — *Interquartile Range — the spread of the middle 50% of data.*

MAD — *Mean Absolute Deviation — average distance from the mean.*

My Progress Log

Track your work through every chapter.

This book belongs to: ______________________________

	Chapter	Topics	Score
1	Ratios, Rates, and Percents	10 topics	________ / ____
2	The Number System	11 topics	________ / ____
3	Expressions and Equations	10 topics	________ / ____
4	Geometry: Area, Surface Area, & Vol.	6 topics	________ / ____
5	Statistics and Data	7 topics	________ / ____

◎ My Weekly Goal

I want to finish _______ topics each week.

My target date to complete this workbook: ____________________

Notes & Topics to Review

Table of Contents

Here's what we'll explore together!

1 Ratios, Rates, and Percents 2

2 The Number System 45

3 Expressions and Equations 89

4 Geometry: Area, Surface Area, and Volume 119

5 Statistics and Data 138

Answer Key 161

Let's learn and have fun!

CHAPTER

1

Ratios, Rates, and Percents

What's Inside

1.1 What Is a Ratio? 3

1.2 Using Ratio Language 8

1.3 What Is a Rate? 13

1.4 Finding the Unit Rate 18

1.5 Tables of Equivalent Ratios 23

1.6 Graphing Ratios 30

1.7 What Is a Percent? 33

1.8 Solving Percent Problems 36

1.9 Solving Rate and Ratio Word Problems 39

1.10 Converting Measurement Units 42

1.1 What Is a Ratio?

What Is a Ratio?

Learning Goals

- *Understand that a ratio compares two quantities*
- *Write ratios in three different forms*
- *Identify and describe ratios in everyday situations*

Ratios Are Everywhere

*Imagine you're making a fruit smoothie. The recipe says to use 2 cups of strawberries for every 3 cups of banana. That "2 for every 3" is a **ratio** — and you use ratios all the time, whether you realize it or not!*

What Is a Ratio?

*A **ratio** is a comparison of two quantities. It tells you how much of one thing there is compared to another.*

For example, if a bag has 5 red marbles and 3 blue marbles, you can compare them with a ratio:

- *The ratio of red to blue is 5 to 3.*
- *The ratio of blue to red is 3 to 5.*

Order matters! The ratio 5 to 3 is NOT the same as 3 to 5.

> *Think of a ratio like a recipe — the order of the ingredients matters! "2 cups flour to 1 cup sugar" is very different from "1 cup flour to 2 cups sugar."*

Three Ways to Write a Ratio

You can write the same ratio in three different forms:

Words	Colon	Fraction
5 to 3	$5:3$	$\frac{5}{3}$

All three mean the same thing: for every 5 of the first quantity, there are 3 of the second.

TIP

When you write a ratio as a fraction, it does NOT mean "5 divided by 3." It's still a comparison. The context tells you it's a ratio, not a division problem.

Writing Ratios from a Picture

A parking lot has 4 trucks and 7 cars.

Write the ratio of trucks to cars in three ways.

Solution:

1. *Identify the two quantities: trucks $= 4$, cars $= 7$.*
2. *Write the ratio in order — trucks first, cars second.*

Words	Colon	Fraction
4 to 7	$4:7$	$\frac{4}{7}$

What about the ratio of cars to trucks?

Answer: 7 to 4, $7 : 4$, $\frac{7}{4}$

Part-to-Part vs. Part-to-Whole

A classroom has 12 boys and 18 girls.

Part-to-Part:

- *Boys to girls:* $12 : 18$
- *Girls to boys:* $18 : 12$

Part-to-Whole:

- *Total students:* $12 + 18 = 30$
- *Boys to total:* $12 : 30$
- *Girls to total:* $18 : 30$

Part-to-part *ratios compare one part of a group to another part.*

Part-to-whole *ratios compare one part to the entire group.*

Always read the problem carefully to know which type is being asked for!

The same situation can give you many different ratios depending on what you're comparing.

Identifying Ratios in Real Life

A pizza shop sells 3 cheese pizzas for every 2 pepperoni pizzas. On Saturday they sold 15 cheese pizzas. How many pepperoni pizzas did they sell?

Solution:

1. *The ratio of cheese to pepperoni is* $3:2$.
2. *They sold* 15 *cheese pizzas. That's* $15 \div 3 = 5$ *groups of* 3.
3. *So there must be* 5 *groups of* 2 *pepperoni pizzas:* $5 \times 2 = 10$.

Answer: They sold 10 pepperoni pizzas.

Watch the Order!

If a problem says "the ratio of cats to dogs is $3:5$*," that means:*

- *Cats* $= 3$, *Dogs* $= 5$ ✓
- *Dogs* $= 3$, *Cats* $= 5$ ***WRONG!***

Always match the first number to the first thing named, and the second number to the second thing named.

What Is a Ratio? — Practice

Write the Ratio

A bag contains 6 apples and 10 oranges. Write each ratio in all three forms (words, colon, fraction).

1. *The ratio of apples to oranges.*
2. *The ratio of oranges to apples.*
3. *The ratio of apples to total fruit*

Read and Write Ratios

4. *A recipe uses 3 eggs and 5 cups of flour. What is the ratio of eggs to flour?*
5. *In a class, there are 14 students who walk to school and 8 who ride the bus. Write the ratio of bus riders to walkers as a fraction.*
6. *A team won 9 games and lost 6 games. Write the ratio of wins to total games played.*

Apply It

7. *A store sells phones and tablets in a ratio of $5 : 2$. If the store sold 20 phones, how many tablets did it sell?*
8. *At a concert, the ratio of adults to children is $7 : 3$. If there are 21 adults, how many children are there?*

You just learned ratios — one of the most useful ideas in all of math!

1.2 Using Ratio Language

Using Ratio Language

Learning Goals

- *Use phrases like "for every," "for each," and "per" to describe ratios*
- *Connect ratio language to math expressions*
- *Read and draw tape diagrams to represent ratios*

I ran 3 laps for every 2 laps my friend ran.

Owl

What does "for every" actually mean?

You

It means that ***each time*** *I complete 3 laps, my friend completes 2. The two amounts always stay in that same relationship!*

Owl

Ratio Language

When you describe a ratio, you use special phrases to show the relationship between two quantities:

- ***"for every"** — For every 3 red beads, there are 5 blue beads.*
- ***"for each"** — For each dollar you save, your parents add 2 dollars.*
- ***"per"** — The car travels 60 miles per hour.*
- ***"to"** — The ratio of wins to losses is 4 to 1.*
- ***"out of"** — 7 out of 10 students prefer pizza (part-to-whole).*

Each phrase connects words to the math behind ratios.

Translating Words to Ratios

*A bakery makes 5 chocolate chip cookies **for every** 2 oatmeal cookies.*

Solution:

1. *Identify the two quantities: chocolate chip $= 5$, oatmeal $= 2$.*
2. *"For every" tells us this is a ratio.*
3. *Write the ratio: $5 : 2$ (chocolate chip to oatmeal).*

We can also say:

- *The ratio of chocolate chip to oatmeal is 5 to 2.*
- *There are $\frac{5}{2}$ times as many chocolate chip cookies as oatmeal cookies.*
- *For each oatmeal cookie, there are $2\frac{1}{2}$ chocolate chip cookies.*

Tape Diagrams

*A **tape diagram** uses rectangular bars to show a ratio visually. Each bar is divided into equal parts.*

***Example:** The ratio of cats to dogs at a shelter is $3 : 4$.*

Each small rectangle represents the same amount. Cats have 3 parts, dogs have 4 parts. Together that's $3+4=7$ parts.

Using a Tape Diagram

The ratio of fiction to nonfiction books on a shelf is $2:5$. There are 35 books total. How many are fiction?

Solution:

1. *Draw a tape diagram: 2 parts for fiction, 5 parts for nonfiction.*
2. *Total parts: $2+5=7$.*
3. *Each part represents: $35 \div 7 = 5$ books.*
4. *Fiction: $2 \times 5 = 10$ books.*

Answer:* *There are 10 fiction books.

> *"Tape diagrams are like a superpower for ratio problems. When you're stuck, draw one — it makes the relationship visible!"*

Writing Ratio Statements

A store sells 8 bottles of water for every 3 bottles of juice.

Write three different ratio statements about this situation.

Solution:

1. **Part-to-part:** *For every 8 waters, there are 3 juices. (Ratio: $8 : 3$)*
2. **Part-to-whole:** *8 out of every 11 drinks sold are water. (Ratio: $8 : 11$)*
3. **Multiplicative:** *Water sales are $\frac{8}{3}$ times juice sales.*

Spot the Error

A Common Mistake with "Out Of" ***A sports team wins 4 out of every 7 games.***

~~The ratio of wins to losses is $4 : 7$.~~ $\longrightarrow$ ________________

What went wrong? *"4 out of 7" is a* **part-to-whole** *ratio. The team wins 4 and loses $7 - 4 = 3$.*

The correct ratio of wins to losses is $4 : 3$.

Using Ratio Language — Practice

Translate Words to Ratios

1. *A pet shelter has* 6 *cats* **for every** 5 *dogs. Write the ratio of cats to dogs.*

2. *A student reads* 4 *pages* **per** *minute. Write the ratio of pages to minutes.*

3. *In a trail mix,* 3 **out of** *every* 8 *pieces are raisins. Write the ratio of raisins to total pieces.*

4. *In the trail mix from Problem 3, what is the ratio of raisins to non-raisins?*

Tape Diagrams

5. *The ratio of boys to girls on a bus is* $3:5$*. There are* 40 *students total. How many boys are on the bus?*

6. *A farmer plants corn and beans in a ratio of* $4:1$*. If the farmer plants* 60 *rows total, how many rows are corn?*

Apply It

7. *Write a real-world situation that matches the ratio* $2:7$*.*

8. *A coach keeps a ratio of* 5 *practice days* **for every** 1 *game day. In a* 24*-day period, how many are practice days and how many are game days?*

You're speaking the language of ratios like a pro!

1.3 What Is a Rate?

What Is a Rate?

Learning Goals

- *Understand that a rate compares two quantities with different units*
- *Identify the units in a rate*
- *Write rates clearly using "per" language*

Rates Rule Your Life

You probably already think about rates every day:

- *Your phone plan:* 5 *GB* ***per*** *month*
- *A road trip:* 65 *miles* ***per*** *hour*
- *Grocery shopping:* $2.50 ***per*** *pound of chicken*
- *Your favorite game:* 120 *points* ***per*** *level*

Every time you see the word "per," you're looking at a rate!

What Is a Rate?

A ***rate*** *is a special kind of ratio that compares two quantities measured in* ***different units****.*

Example	*Quantity 1*	*Quantity 2*
300 *miles in* 5 *hours*	*miles*	*hours*
$12 *for* 4 *sandwiches*	*dollars*	*sandwiches*
150 *words in* 3 *minutes*	*words*	*minutes*

If both quantities use the SAME unit (like 3 boys to 5 girls — both are people), it's just a ratio. If the units are DIFFERENT, it's a rate.

Ratio	Rate
*Compares quantities with the **same** or similar units.*	*Compares quantities with **different** units.*
Examples:	*Examples:*
• 3 *cats to* 5 *dogs*	• $15 *per hour*
• 12 *boys to* 18 *girls*	• 60 *miles per hour*
• 2 *wins to* 1 *loss*	• 3 *apples per bag*

“Here's a quick test: if you can say "per" between the two quantities and it makes sense, it's a rate! "Miles per hour" — yep, that's a rate.”

Identifying Rates

Which of the following are rates? Identify the two units in each rate.

1. 5 *red cards to* 3 *blue cards*
2. 240 *heartbeats in* 4 *minutes*
3. $36 *for* 9 *gallons of gas*

4. 7 boys out of 20 students

Solution:

1. **Not a rate** — both are cards (same type of unit). This is a ratio.
2. **Rate** — heartbeats and minutes are different units. Rate: 240 heartbeats per 4 minutes.
3. **Rate** — dollars and gallons are different units. Rate: \$36 per 9 gallons.
4. **Not a rate** — boys and students are the same type (people). This is a part-to-whole ratio.

Writing Rates

A printer prints 120 pages in 8 minutes. Write this as a rate.

Solution:

1. Identify the quantities and their units: 120 pages, 8 minutes.
2. Write the rate with "per": 120 pages per 8 minutes, or 120 pages/8 minutes.
3. As a fraction: $\frac{120 \text{ pages}}{8 \text{ minutes}}$.

Answer: $\frac{120 \text{ pages}}{8 \text{ minutes}}$ or 120 pages per 8 minutes

TIP

Always include the units when you write a rate. Writing just "120 to 8" loses the meaning. Writing "120 pages per 8 minutes" tells the whole story.

How to Write a Rate

1. Identify the two quantities and their units.

2. *Check that the units are **different** (that's what makes it a rate).*
3. *Write the rate using "per" or as a fraction with units.*

What Is a Rate? — Practice

Rate or Ratio?

*Decide whether each situation describes a **rate** or a **ratio**. Write "Rate" or "Ratio."*

1. 5 touchdowns in 3 games
2. 4 red shirts to 6 blue shirts
3. 200 calories in 1 granola bar
4. 9 girls out of 15 students

Write the Rate

5. A car travels 180 miles in 3 hours. Write this as a rate with units.
6. A factory makes 500 toys in 4 days. Write this as a rate with units.

Apply It

7. A runner completes 6 laps in 12 minutes. A cyclist completes 6 laps in 8 minutes. Who is faster? Explain using rates.
8. Name a real-life rate you used or saw today. Write it with units.

You can spot rates everywhere now — that's a skill worth having!

1.4 Finding the Unit Rate

Finding the Unit Rate

Learning Goals

- *Understand that a unit rate has a denominator of* 1
- *Find unit rates by dividing*
- *Use unit rates to solve real-world problems like unit pricing and speed*

At the Grocery Store

You're comparing two brands of orange juice:

- *Brand A:* 64 *oz for* $\$4.80$
- *Brand B:* 48 *oz for* $\$3.36$

Which is the better deal? You can't tell just by looking — you need to find the ***unit rate****.*

What Is a Unit Rate?

A ***unit rate*** *is a rate where the second quantity is exactly* 1*.*

Rate	*Unit Rate*
300 *miles in* 5 *hours*	60 *miles per* 1 *hour* (60 ***mph***)
$12 *for* 4 *pounds*	$3 *per* 1 *pound* (**$3/lb**)
120 *words in* 2 *minutes*	60 *words per* 1 *minute* (60 ***wpm***)

To find a unit rate, divide the first quantity by the second quantity.

How to Find a Unit Rate

1. *Write the rate as a fraction with units.*
2. *Divide the numerator by the denominator.*
3. *Write the answer with "per 1" or just "per" and the unit.*

Finding a Unit Rate

A car travels 225 *miles on* 9 *gallons of gas. Find the unit rate.*

Solution:

1. *Write the rate:* $\frac{225 \text{ miles}}{9 \text{ gallons}}$
2. *Divide:* $225 \div 9 = 25$
3. *Write the unit rate:* 25 *miles per gallon*

Answer: 25 ***miles per gallon (mpg)***

Unit Pricing — Which Is the Better Deal?

Let's solve the grocery store problem from earlier.

- *Brand A:* 64 *oz for* $\$4.80$
- *Brand B:* 48 *oz for* $\$3.36$

Find the price per ounce for each:

Brand A: $\$4.80 \div 64 = \$0.075$ *per ounce*

Brand B: $\$3.36 \div 48 = \$0.07$ *per ounce*

> ***Answer:*** ***Brand B is the better deal at*** $\$0.07$ ***per ounce.***

> *"Unit pricing is how smart shoppers compare! Three different-sized boxes of cereal? Find the price per ounce and the cheapest one jumps right out."*

Speed as a Unit Rate

A cheetah runs 700 *meters in* 28 *seconds. A greyhound runs* 400 *meters in* 20 *seconds. Which animal is faster?*

Solution:

Cheetah: $700 \div 28 = 25$ *meters per second*

Greyhound: $400 \div 20 = 20$ *meters per second*

> ***Answer:*** ***The cheetah is faster at*** 25 ***meters per second.***

Spot the Error

Dividing the Wrong Way A recipe uses 6 cups of flour for 2 batches. Find the unit rate.

~~$2 \div 6 = 0.33$ *batches per cup*~~ $\longrightarrow$ ________________

The student divided the denominator by the numerator. The question asks for cups ***per batch****, so divide cups by batches:*

$6 \div 2 = 3$ *cups per batch* ✓

Tip: *Ask yourself: "Per ONE of what?" The "what" goes on the bottom.*

TIP

Not sure which number to divide by? Look for the word "per." Whatever comes ***after*** *"per" is the unit you want to be 1. Miles* ***per hour*** *means divide miles by hours.*

Finding the Unit Rate — Practice

Find the Unit Rate

1. A swimmer completes 20 laps in 10 minutes. What is the unit rate?
2. A factory produces 450 cans in 6 hours. How many cans per hour?
3. You earn $84 for 7 hours of work. What is your hourly rate?
4. A jet flies 2,400 miles in 4 hours. What is its speed in miles per hour?

Unit Pricing

5. A 12-pack of sparkling water costs $5.40 and a 6-pack costs $3.00. Which is the better buy?
6. A 16 oz jar of peanut butter costs $4.00 and a 28 oz jar costs $5.60. Find the unit price of each and identify the better deal.

Apply It

7. A car's GPS shows it traveled 168 miles on 5.6 gallons of gas. What is the car's fuel efficiency in miles per gallon?
8. Maya reads 54 pages in 1.5 hours. Ethan reads 80 pages in 2 hours. Who reads faster? Justify your answer using unit rates.

Unit rates make comparing things super simple. Nice work!

★ 1.5 Tables of Equivalent Ratios ★

Tables of Equivalent Ratios

◎ Learning Goals

- Build ratio tables by multiplying or dividing both quantities
- Use ratio tables to find missing values
- Understand that equivalent ratios form the same relationship

If making 1 batch of lemonade requires 2 cups of lemon juice and 5 cups of water, how much do I need for 4 batches?

Owl

Just multiply both amounts by 4!

You

*Exactly! And a **ratio table** organizes all those equivalent amounts in one place.*

Owl

Equivalent Ratios

*Two ratios are **equivalent** if you can multiply (or divide) both parts of one ratio by the same number to get the other.*

$$2:5 \quad \longrightarrow \quad \times 3 \quad \longrightarrow \quad 6:15$$

So $2:5$ and $6:15$ are equivalent ratios. They represent the same relationship.

Multiplying or dividing both parts of a ratio by the same nonzero number gives an equivalent ratio.

Ratio Tables

*A **ratio table** lists pairs of numbers that all share the same ratio. You build one by multiplying (or dividing) both columns by the same number.*

Lemonade recipe: 2 cups lemon juice for every 5 cups water.

Lemon Juice (cups)	*Water (cups)*
2	5
4	10
6	15
8	20
10	25

Every row shows an equivalent ratio: $2:5 = 4:10 = 6:15 = 8:20 = 10:25$.

How to Build a Ratio Table

1. *Start with the given ratio.*
2. *Multiply **both** values by $2, 3, 4, \dots$ to find more equivalent ratios.*
3. *To go backward (smaller values), divide both by the same number.*
4. *To find a specific missing value, figure out the multiplier from the column you know.*

Finding Missing Values in a Ratio Table

Complete the ratio table.

Pencils	*Erasers*
3	2
9	?
?	10
18	?

Solution:

1. *Row 2: Pencils went from 3 to 9, so we multiplied by 3. Erasers: $2 \times 3 = 6$.*
2. *Row 3: Erasers went from 2 to 10, so we multiplied by 5. Pencils: $3 \times 5 = 15$.*
3. *Row 4: Pencils went from 3 to 18, so we multiplied by 6. Erasers: $2 \times 6 = 12$.*

Pencils	*Erasers*	*Multiplier*
3	2	$\times 1$
9	6	$\times 3$
15	10	$\times 5$
18	12	$\times 6$

“Think of a ratio table as a recipe scaler. You're making the same recipe — just in bigger or smaller batches!”

Using a Ratio Table to Solve a Problem

A store sells notebooks in packs. The ratio of blue notebooks to red notebooks is $4 : 3$. If you buy 20 blue notebooks, how many red notebooks do you get?

Solution:

Build a ratio table:

Blue	*Red*
4	3
8	6
12	9
16	12
20	15

Or use the shortcut: $20 \div 4 = 5$, so we multiplied by 5. Red $= 3 \times 5 = 15$.

Answer: You get 15 red notebooks.

Watch Out!

A common mistake is to add the same number to both parts instead of ***multiplying****.*

$3:5 \xrightarrow{+3} 6:8$ ***WRONG!*** $6:8$ *is NOT equivalent to* $3:5$.

$3:5 \xrightarrow{\times 2} 6:10$ ✓ *This is correct!*

Tables of Equivalent Ratios — Practice

Complete the Table

1. Complete the ratio table for the ratio $5 : 2$.

A	B
5	2
10	______
______	8
25	______

2. Complete the ratio table for the ratio $7 : 3$.

X	Y
7	3
14	______
______	12
35	______

Equivalent or Not?

3. Are $6 : 9$ and $14 : 21$ equivalent ratios? Explain.

4. Are $5 : 8$ and $15 : 20$ equivalent ratios? Explain.

Apply It

5. *A smoothie recipe uses fruit and yogurt in a* $3:2$ *ratio. If you use* 12 *cups of fruit, how many cups of yogurt do you need?*

6. *A class has a boy-to-girl ratio of* $5:7$*. If there are* 35 *girls, how many students are in the class total?*

7. *A painter mixes blue and white paint in a* $2:9$ *ratio. She needs* 33 *total cups of paint. How many cups of each color does she need?*

Ratio tables are one of your most powerful tools — use them!

1.6 Graphing Ratios

Learning Goals

- *Plot ratio pairs as points on a coordinate plane*
- *Recognize that equivalent ratios form a straight line through the origin*
- *Use a graph to find missing values*

From Table to Graph

You can turn a ratio table into a graph. Each row becomes a point (x, y).

If $y = 3x$, *the points are* $(1, 3)$, $(2, 6)$, $(3, 9)$, $(4, 12)$.
All these points line up in a straight line through $(0, 0)$.

Equivalent ratios always make a straight line through the origin $(0, 0)$.

Plot and Predict

Juice costs \$2 *per bottle. Make a table and graph for* 1–4 *bottles. How much for* 5 *bottles?*

Solution:

1. *Table:* $(1, 2)$, $(2, 4)$, $(3, 6)$, $(4, 8)$.
2. *Plot these points. They form a straight line.*
3. *Extend the line to* $x = 5$. *Read* $y = 10$.

Answer: 5 ***bottles cost*** $\$10$.

"If your points don't line up, double-check your table. Equivalent ratios ***always*** *make a straight line!"*

Graphing Practice

Plot and Answer

1. A car goes 30 miles each hour. List the four points you would plot for hours 1 through 4.
2. Does the point $(3, 9)$ belong on the graph of the ratio $1 : 3$?
3. The points $(2, 5)$ and $(4, 10)$ are on a line. What is the ratio?

Think Deeper

4. Two ratio graphs both go through the origin. Line A goes through $(1, 4)$. Line B goes through $(1, 3)$. Which line is steeper?
5. A graph of equivalent ratios can be a curved line. True ○ False ○

1.7 What Is a Percent?

Learning Goals

- Understand that percent means "per 100"
- Convert between percents, fractions, and decimals
- Model percents using grids

Percent means "per 100." The symbol % means "out of 100."

Percents, Fractions, and Decimals

All three show parts of a whole:

Percent	Fraction	Decimal
25%	$\frac{25}{100} = \frac{1}{4}$	0.25
50%	$\frac{50}{100} = \frac{1}{2}$	0.50
75%	$\frac{75}{100} = \frac{3}{4}$	0.75
100%	$\frac{100}{100} = 1$	1.00

To convert a percent to a decimal, divide by 100 (move the decimal point two places left).

Shade a Grid

Show 40% on a 10×10 grid.

Solution:

1. *A 10×10 grid has 100 squares.*
2. *40% means 40 out of 100.*
3. *Shade 40 squares.*

Answer: Shade 40 out of 100 squares. As a fraction: $\frac{40}{100} = \frac{2}{5}$. As a decimal: 0.40.

TIP
Think of a percent grid like a 100-square chocolate bar. 40% means you ate 40 squares!

Percent Practice

Convert

1. Write 60% as a fraction and a decimal.
2. Write $\frac{3}{4}$ as a percent.
3. Write 0.15 as a percent.

Apply

4. A test has 100 questions. Emma got 88 correct. What percent did she get right?
5. A store has 200 items. 50% of them are on sale. How many items are on sale?
6. Which is greater: 30% or $\frac{1}{4}$?

You now speak the language of percents — great job!

1.8 Solving Percent Problems

Learning Goals

- Find a percent of a number (e.g., 30% of 50)
- Find the whole when given a part and a percent
- Estimate to check if percent answers are reasonable

Finding a Percent of a Number

To find a percent of a number, **multiply**.

Part = Percent × Whole

Write the percent as a decimal or fraction first:

- 20% of $60 \rightarrow 0.20 \times 60 = 12$
- 25% of $80 \rightarrow \frac{1}{4} \times 80 = 20$

Pick whichever form (decimal or fraction) makes the math easiest.

Find the Part and the Whole

Part A:

What is 15% of 200?

$0.15 \times 200 = 30.$

Answer: 30

Part B:

40% of what number is 28?

Solution:

1. *Set up:* $0.40 \times ? = 28.$
2. *Divide:* $28 \div 0.40 = 70.$

Answer: *The whole is* 70.

“Quick check — 50% is always half, 10% is always one-tenth. Use these to estimate!”

Percent Problems

Find the Percent of a Number

1. 30% *of* $90 =$ __________
2. 75% *of* $200 =$ __________
3. 10% *of* $350 =$ __________

Find the Whole

4. 25% *of what number is* 20?
5. 50% *of what number is* 33?

Word Problem

6. *A jacket costs* $\$80$. *It is* 25% *off. How much do you save? How much do you pay?*

1.9 Solving Rate and Ratio Word Problems

Learning Goals

- *Choose the right tool (tables, tape diagrams, equations) to solve ratio problems*
- *Show clear reasoning with units and steps*
- *Solve multi-step rate and ratio problems*

Pick a Strategy

You now have several tools. Pick the one that fits:

- ***Ratio table** — great when you need to scale up or down step by step.*
- ***Tape diagram** — great for part-to-part or part-to-whole problems.*
- ***Unit rate** — great when you need "how much for one?"*
- ***Equation** — great when you can set up equal ratios:* $\frac{a}{b} = \frac{c}{d}$.

Ratio Table Strategy

A recipe makes 12 *cookies using* 2 *eggs. How many eggs to make* 42 *cookies?*

Solution:

1. *Unit rate:* $12 \div 2 = 6$ *cookies per egg.*
2. $42 \div 6 = 7$ *eggs.*

Answer: 7 **eggs**

Tape Diagram Strategy

Boys and girls are in a $3:5$ ratio. There are 40 students. How many boys?

Boys:

Girls:

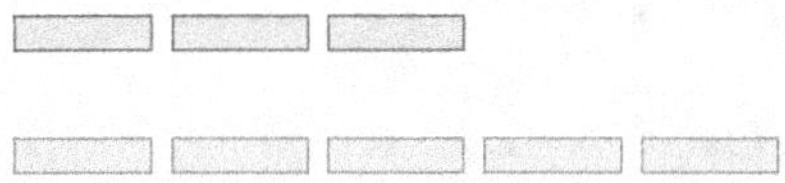

Total parts: $3+5=8$.

Each part: $40 \div 8 = 5$.

Boys: $3 \times 5 = 15$.

Answer: 15 ***boys***

TIP

Always write your units! "7" alone is unclear. "7 eggs" is a complete answer.

Word Problem Practice

1. *A car travels* 180 *miles in* 3 *hours. At the same rate, how far will it go in* 7 *hours?*
2. *A paint mix uses red and white in a* $2:7$ *ratio. You need* 36 *cups total. How much red? How much white?*
3. *Three friends share a prize in a* $1:2:3$ *ratio. The prize is* $\$120$. *How much does each person get?*
4. *A map scale says* 1 *cm* $= 5$ *km. Two cities are* 8 *cm apart on the map. What is the real distance?*
5. *A garden uses* 3 *bags of soil for every* 4 *flower beds. How many bags for* 20 *flower beds?*

1.10 Converting Measurement Units

Learning Goals

- *Use ratio reasoning to convert between measurement units*
- *Convert within the same system (inches to feet, grams to kilograms)*
- *Track units to avoid mistakes*

Unit Conversion Is a Ratio

Converting units is just using a ratio. Every conversion is a rate:

- 1 *foot* $= 12$ *inches* $\rightarrow$ *ratio of* $1:12$
- 1 *meter* $= 100$ *centimeters* $\rightarrow$ *ratio of* $1:100$
- 1 *hour* $= 60$ *minutes* $\rightarrow$ *ratio of* $1:60$

Bigger unit $\rightarrow$ ***smaller unit:*** *multiply.*

Smaller unit $\rightarrow$ ***bigger unit:*** *divide.*

Convert Using Ratios

Bigger to Smaller:

Convert 3.5 *hours to minutes.*

1 *hour* $= 60$ *minutes. Bigger* $\rightarrow$ *smaller means multiply:* $3.5 \times 60 = 210$.

Answer: 3.5 ***hours*** $=$ 210 ***minutes***

Smaller to Bigger:

Convert 450 centimeters to meters.

1 *meter* = 100 *cm. Smaller* → *bigger means divide:* $450 \div 100 = 4.5$.

Answer: 450 ***cm*** = 4.5 ***m***

"*Multiply to go small, divide to go big. The number gets bigger when the unit gets smaller!*"

Unit Conversion Practice

Convert

1. 5 *feet* = __________ *inches*
2. 240 *minutes* = __________ *hours*
3. 3 *kilometers* = __________ *meters*
4. 2,500 *grams* = __________ *kilograms*

Word Problems

5. *A movie is* 135 *minutes long. How many hours and minutes is that?*
6. *A ribbon is* 2.5 *yards long. How many inches is that? (*1 *yard* = 36 *inches)*

CHAPTER

2

The Number System

What's Inside

2.1 Dividing Fractions by Fractions 46

2.2 Multi-Digit Division 51

2.3 Decimal Operations 56

2.4 Greatest Common Factor and Least Common Multiple 62

2.5 The Distributive Property with Common Factors 68

2.6 Understanding Positive and Negative Numbers 71

2.7 Opposites and Absolute Value 74

2.8 Rational Numbers on the Number Line 77

2.9 The Coordinate Plane 80

2.10 Comparing and Ordering Rational Numbers 83

2.11 Distance on the Coordinate Plane 86

2.1 Dividing Fractions by Fractions

Dividing Fractions by Fractions

Learning Goals

- *Understand what it means to divide a fraction by a fraction*
- *Use the "Keep–Change–Flip" method to divide fractions*
- *Connect fraction division to real-world situations*
- *Check your answers using multiplication*

When Do You Divide Fractions?

You have $\frac{3}{4}$ *of a pizza left. You want to split it equally among friends so each person gets* $\frac{1}{4}$ *of the whole pizza. How many people can you feed?*

That's $\frac{3}{4} \div \frac{1}{4}$ *— and the answer is* 3 *people. You just divided a fraction by a fraction!*

What Does Fraction Division Mean?

When you divide by a fraction, you're asking: **"How many of this fraction fit into that amount?"**

$\frac{3}{4} \div \frac{1}{4}$ *means: "How many* $\frac{1}{4}$*'s are in* $\frac{3}{4}$*?"*

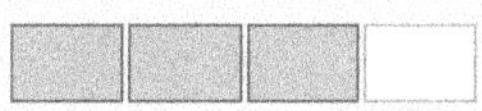

You can count: there are 3 *pieces of size* $\frac{1}{4}$ *in* $\frac{3}{4}$*. So* $\frac{3}{4} \div \frac{1}{4} = 3$*.*

Keep–Change–Flip (Dividing Fractions)

1. **Keep** the first fraction exactly as it is.
2. **Change** the division sign (÷) to multiplication (×).
3. **Flip** the second fraction (swap the numerator and denominator). This flipped fraction is called the **reciprocal**.
4. Multiply straight across: numerators together, denominators together.
5. Simplify if possible.

> “ The **reciprocal** of $\frac{2}{3}$ is $\frac{3}{2}$. Just flip it! Every fraction has a reciprocal — except 0. ”

Divide $\frac{2}{3} \div \frac{4}{5}$

Solution:

1. **Keep** the first fraction: $\frac{2}{3}$
2. **Change** $\div$ to $\times$
3. **Flip** $\frac{4}{5}$ to get $\frac{5}{4}$
4. Multiply: $\frac{2}{3} \times \frac{5}{4} = \frac{2 \times 5}{3 \times 4} = \frac{10}{12}$
5. Simplify: $\frac{10}{12} = \frac{5}{6}$

Answer: $\frac{2}{3} \div \frac{4}{5} = \frac{5}{6}$

TIP

To check your answer, multiply it by the divisor. If you get back the dividend, you're correct!
$\frac{5}{6} \times \frac{4}{5} = \frac{20}{30} = \frac{2}{3}$ ✓

A Real-World Problem

A ribbon is $\frac{7}{8}$ of a yard long. You need pieces that are each $\frac{1}{4}$ of a yard. How many pieces can you cut?

Solution:

1. *Write the division:* $\frac{7}{8} \div \frac{1}{4}$
2. *Keep–Change–Flip:* $\frac{7}{8} \times \frac{4}{1}$
3. *Multiply:* $\frac{7 \times 4}{8 \times 1} = \frac{28}{8}$
4. *Simplify:* $\frac{28}{8} = \frac{7}{2} = 3\frac{1}{2}$

Answer: ***You can cut 3 full pieces (with some ribbon left over).***

Spot the Error

What Went Wrong? Maya solved $\frac{3}{5} \div \frac{2}{7}$ like this:

"I'll flip the first fraction: $\frac{5}{3} \times \frac{2}{7} = \frac{10}{21}$"

What did Maya do wrong? ______________________________

The correct answer is: _______________

*Maya flipped the wrong fraction! You always flip the **second** fraction (the one you're dividing by). The correct work is:*
$\frac{3}{5} \times \frac{7}{2} = \frac{21}{10} = 2\frac{1}{10}$

Dividing a Whole Number by a Fraction

How many $\frac{1}{3}$-cup servings are in 4 cups of soup?

Solution:

1. *Write 4 as a fraction:* $\frac{4}{1}$
2. *Set up:* $\frac{4}{1} \div \frac{1}{3}$
3. *Keep–Change–Flip:* $\frac{4}{1} \times \frac{3}{1} = \frac{12}{1} = 12$

Answer:* *There are 12 servings.

Remember!

- *Dividing by a fraction less than 1 gives you a **bigger** answer.*
- *Dividing by a fraction greater than 1 gives you a **smaller** answer.*
- *Always simplify your final answer.*
- *Check by multiplying: answer $\times$ divisor $=$ dividend.*

Dividing Fractions — Practice

Divide and Simplify

1. $\frac{1}{2} \div \frac{1}{4} =$ ________

2. $\frac{3}{5} \div \frac{1}{2} =$ ________

3. $\frac{5}{6} \div \frac{2}{3} =$ ________

4. $\frac{4}{9} \div \frac{2}{3} =$ ________

Whole Numbers and Fractions

5. $3 \div \frac{1}{5} =$ ________

6. $\frac{7}{8} \div 2 =$ ________

Word Problems

7. *A trail mix recipe needs $\frac{3}{4}$ cup of raisins. Each scoop holds $\frac{1}{8}$ cup. How many scoops do you need?*

8. *A board is $\frac{5}{6}$ of a foot long. You cut it into pieces that are each $\frac{1}{3}$ of a foot. How many pieces do you get?*

Challenge!

1. *You have $\frac{2}{3}$ of a gallon of paint. Each wall needs $\frac{1}{6}$ of a gallon. How many walls can you paint? If a room has 4 walls, do you have enough paint for the whole room?*

2.2 Multi-Digit Division

Multi-Digit Division

Learning Goals

- *Divide multi-digit whole numbers using the standard algorithm*
- *Estimate quotients before dividing*
- *Check answers using multiplication*

I can divide by one-digit numbers, but what about dividing by bigger numbers like 24 or 36?

Alex

Same idea — just more steps! Let's walk through it.

Mia

Long Division Steps

1. **Divide** — *How many times does the divisor go into the current digits?*
2. **Multiply** — *Divisor × your quotient digit.*
3. **Subtract** — *Subtract the product from the current number.*
4. **Bring down** — *Bring down the next digit.*

5 **Repeat** until there are no more digits to bring down.

> Remember the phrase: **"Does McDonald's Sell Burgers Raw?"** — Divide, Multiply, Subtract, Bring down, Repeat!

Divide $846 \div 18$

Step by Step:

1. **Estimate first:** $846 \div 18 \approx 800 \div 20 = 40$. So the answer should be close to 40.
2. **Divide:** 18 goes into 84 how many times? $18 \times 4 = 72$ and $18 \times 5 = 90$ (too big). Write 4 above the 4 in 846.
3. **Multiply:** $4 \times 18 = 72$
4. **Subtract:** $84 - 72 = 12$
5. **Bring down** the 6: now you have 126.
6. **Divide:** 18 goes into 126 how many times? $18 \times 7 = 126$. Write 7.
7. **Multiply:** $7 \times 18 = 126$
8. **Subtract:** $126 - 126 = 0$. No remainder!

Answer: $846 \div 18 = 47$

Check: $47 \times 18 = 846$ ✓

Why Estimate First?

Estimating before you divide helps you:

- Know roughly what to expect (so you catch big mistakes).

- *Choose better quotient digits during long division.*
- *Build strong number sense.*

Quick estimation trick: *Round both numbers to "friendly" numbers, then divide.*

$$4{,}356 \div 52 \approx 4{,}000 \div 50 = 80$$

Division with a Remainder

Divide $1{,}537 \div 24$.

Solution:

1. ***Estimate:*** $1{,}537 \div 24 \approx 1{,}500 \div 25 = 60$
2. 24 *into* 15*? Doesn't go. Try* 153*:* $24 \times 6 = 144$*. Write* 6*.*
3. *Subtract:* $153 - 144 = 9$*. Bring down* 7*: now* 97*.*
4. 24 *into* 97*:* $24 \times 4 = 96$*. Write* 4*.*
5. *Subtract:* $97 - 96 = 1$*. No more digits to bring down.*

Answer: $1{,}537 \div 24 = 64\ \boldsymbol{R}\ 1$

Check: $64 \times 24 + 1 = 1{,}536 + 1 = 1{,}537$ ✓

TIP

Always check: quotient × divisor + remainder = dividend. If it doesn't match, go back and find your mistake!

Remember!

- *The remainder must always be **less than** the divisor.*
- *If your remainder is bigger than the divisor, your quotient digit is too small — try a larger one.*
- *Line up your digits carefully. Sloppy columns cause errors!*

Multi-Digit Division — Practice

Divide Using the Standard Algorithm

1. $756 \div 12 =$ __________
2. $972 \div 27 =$ __________
3. $1{,}248 \div 16 =$ __________
4. $2{,}340 \div 45 =$ __________

Division with Remainders

5. $895 \div 14 =$ __________
6. $3{,}217 \div 38 =$ __________

Word Problems

7. *A school is ordering buses for a field trip. There are 342 students and each bus holds 36 passengers. How many buses are needed?*

8. *A factory makes 2,856 toy cars in 14 hours. How many cars does it make per hour?*

Challenge!

1. *Without doing the full division, explain how you know that* $4{,}753 \div 23$ *has a two-digit quotient (not three digits). Then find the actual answer.*

2.3 Decimal Operations

Decimal Operations

Learning Goals

- Add, subtract, multiply, and divide decimals fluently
- Use place value to line up decimals correctly
- Estimate to check if answers are reasonable

Decimal operations follow the same rules as whole-number operations — you just need to keep track of the decimal point!

Adding and Subtracting Decimals

The key rule: **line up the decimal points**, then add or subtract as usual.

$$\begin{array}{r} 12.350 \\ +\ 4.075 \\ \hline 16.425 \end{array} \qquad \begin{array}{r} 8.200 \\ -\ 3.146 \\ \hline 5.054 \end{array}$$

TIP
Fill in trailing zeros so both numbers have the same number of decimal places. It makes subtraction much easier! 8.2 becomes 8.200.

Multiplying Decimals

*Multiply as if the numbers were whole numbers. Then count the **total decimal places** in both factors and place the decimal point in the product.*

$$2.4 \times 0.13 = ?$$

1. *Ignore the decimals:* $24 \times 13 = 312$
2. *Count decimal places:* 2.4 *has* 1 *place,* 0.13 *has* 2 *places* $\rightarrow$ *total* 3 *places*
3. *Place the decimal:* $312 \rightarrow 0.312$

Answer: $2.4 \times 0.13 = 0.312$

> *Quick check:* 2.4×0.13 *should be less than* 2.4 *(because you're multiplying by something less than 1). Is* $0.312 < 2.4$*? Yes! Makes sense.*

Dividing Decimals

*To divide by a decimal, **move the decimal point** in the divisor to make it a whole number. Move the decimal in the dividend the same number of places.*

$$7.56 \div 0.3$$

1. *Move the decimal in* 0.3 *one place right:* $0.3 \rightarrow 3$

2. *Move the decimal in* 7.56 *one place right:* $7.56 \rightarrow 75.6$
3. *Now divide:* $75.6 \div 3 = 25.2$

Answer: $7.56 \div 0.3 = 25.2$

Putting It All Together

A phone plan costs $\$34.50$ *per month. If you also pay a one-time setup fee of* $\$12.75$*, what is the total cost for* 6 *months?*

Solution:

1. *Monthly cost for* 6 *months:* $34.50 \times 6 = 207.00$
2. *Add the setup fee:* $207.00 + 12.75 = 219.75$

Answer: ***The total cost is*** $\$219.75$.

Spot the Error

A student computed 3.5×2.4 *and got* 84.0.

What went wrong? The student forgot to place the decimal point. $35 \times 24 = 840$*, but there are* 2 *total decimal places* $(1 + 1)$*, so the answer should be* 8.40 *(or* 8.4*).*

Estimate check: $3.5 \times 2.4 \approx 4 \times 2 = 8$*. The answer* 84 *is way too big!*

Remember!

- ***Add/Subtract:*** *Line up the decimal points.*
- ***Multiply:*** *Count total decimal places in both factors.*
- ***Divide:*** *Move the decimal to make the divisor a whole number.*
- ***Always:*** *Estimate first to check if your answer is reasonable.*

Decimal Operations — Practice

Add and Subtract

1. $14.63 + 7.089 =$ __________

2. $50.2 - 13.85 =$ __________

3. $100 - 27.456 =$ __________

4. $3.007 + 12.93 =$ __________

Multiply

5. $6.3 \times 4.1 =$ __________

6. $0.07 \times 0.5 =$ __________

Divide

7. $9.12 \div 0.4 =$ __________

8. $15.6 \div 1.2 =$ __________

Word Problems

9. *You buy* 3 *notebooks at* $\$2.49$ *each and a pen for* $\$1.75$*. What is the total cost?*

10. *A relay team of* 4 *runners finished a race in* 52.8 *seconds total. If each runner ran the same time, how long did each runner take?*

Challenge!

1. *Without a calculator, find* 0.012×0.05 *and explain how you placed the decimal point.*

★ 2.4 Greatest Common Factor and Least Common Multiple ★

Greatest Common Factor and Least Common Multiple

Learning Goals

- *Find the greatest common factor (GCF) of two numbers up to* 100
- *Find the least common multiple (LCM) of two numbers up to* 12
- *Use factor lists and prime factorization*

Vocabulary

Factor — A number that divides evenly into another number. The factors of 12 *are* $1, 2, 3, 4, 6, 12$.

Multiple — The result of multiplying a number by a whole number. Multiples of 4*:* $4, 8, 12, 16, 20, \ldots$

GCF — The ***greatest common factor*** *— the largest factor shared by two numbers.*

LCM — The ***least common multiple*** *— the smallest multiple shared by two numbers (other than* 0*).*

Finding the GCF

To find the GCF of two numbers, list all the factors of each number and pick the ***largest one they share****.*

Find the GCF of 24 ***and*** 36*:*

- *Factors of* 24*:* $1, 2, 3, 4, 6, 8, 12, 24$

- *Factors of* 36: $1, 2, 3, 4, 6, 9, 12, 18, 36$
- *Common factors:* $1, 2, 3, 4, 6, 12$

Answer: ***GCF of*** 24 ***and*** 36 ***is*** 12.

GCF Using Prime Factorization

Find the GCF of 48 *and* 60.

Prime factorizations:

- $48 = 2 \times 2 \times 2 \times 2 \times 3$
- $60 = 2 \times 2 \times 3 \times 5$

Circle the prime factors they ***share***:

- *Shared:* $2 \times 2 \times 3 = 12$

Multiply the shared primes together to get the GCF.

Answer: $\text{GCF}(48, 60) = 12$

"Think of the GCF as the biggest "building block" that fits evenly into both numbers. It's super useful for simplifying fractions!"

Finding the LCM

To find the LCM, list multiples of each number until you find the ***smallest one they share***.

Find the LCM of 6 ***and*** 8:

- *Multiples of* 6: $6, 12, 18,$ **24**$, 30, \ldots$

- *Multiples of 8:* $8, 16, \mathbf{24}, 32, \ldots$

Answer: LCM of 6 and 8 is 24.

LCM Using Prime Factorization

Find the LCM of 9 and 12.

Solution:

1. Prime factorizations: $9 = 3 \times 3$ and $12 = 2 \times 2 \times 3$
2. Take the **highest power** of each prime: 2^2 and 3^2
3. Multiply: $2^2 \times 3^2 = 4 \times 9 = 36$

Answer: $\text{LCM}(9, 12) = 36$

GCF vs. LCM	When to Use Each
GCF is for **splitting things into equal groups**: • Simplifying fractions • Dividing items into equal groups • "What's the most you can split evenly?"	**LCM** is for **finding when things line up**: • Adding fractions (common denominator) • Repeating schedules • "When will they happen at the same time?"

A Real-World GCF Problem

You have 18 apples and 24 granola bars. You want to make gift bags with the same number of apples and the same number of granola bars in each bag, with nothing left over. What is the greatest number of bags you can make?

Solution:

1. Find GCF$(18, 24)$: factors of 18 are $1, 2, 3, 6, 9, 18$; factors of 24 are $1, 2, 3, 4, 6, 8, 12, 24$.
2. GCF $= 6$, so you can make 6 bags.
3. Each bag gets $18 \div 6 = 3$ apples and $24 \div 6 = 4$ granola bars.

Answer: 6 bags (3 apples and 4 granola bars each).

A Real-World LCM Problem

Hot dogs come in packs of 8. Buns come in packs of 6. What is the least number of each you should buy so you have the same number of hot dogs and buns?

Solution:

1. Find LCM$(8, 6)$: multiples of 8 are $8, 16, 24, \ldots$; multiples of 6 are $6, 12, 18, 24, \ldots$
2. LCM $= 24$
3. You need $24 \div 8 = 3$ packs of hot dogs and $24 \div 6 = 4$ packs of buns.

Answer: Buy 3 packs of hot dogs and 4 packs of buns (24 of each).

GCF and LCM – Practice

Find the GCF

1. GCF of 16 and 40: __________
2. GCF of 36 and 54: __________
3. GCF of 28 and 42: __________
4. GCF of 100 and 75: __________

Find the LCM

5. LCM of 4 and 10: __________
6. LCM of 6 and 9: __________
7. LCM of 8 and 12: __________
8. LCM of 5 and 7: __________

Word Problems

9. You have 30 pencils and 48 erasers. You want to put them into identical goodie bags with no items left over. What is the greatest number of bags you can make?

10. Two buses leave the station at the same time. Bus A returns every 12 minutes. Bus B returns every 8 minutes. In how many minutes will they both be at the station again at the same time?

Challenge!

1.

2. The GCF of any number and itself is always that number. True ○ False ○

3.

4. The LCM of two numbers is always bigger than both numbers. **True** ◯ **False** ◯

2.5 The Distributive Property with Common Factors

Learning Goals

- *Rewrite a sum using the distributive property*
- *Factor out the GCF from two numbers*
- *Use the distributive property for mental math*

The Distributive Property

The ***distributive property*** *says:*

$$a(b+c) = a \times b + a \times c$$

You can also go backwards. If two numbers share a common factor, pull it out:

$$36 + 8 = 4(9 + 2)$$

Both 36 *and* 8 *are divisible by* 4*. So factor out the* 4*.*

Factor a Sum

Rewrite $24 + 18$ *using the distributive property.*

Solution:

1. *Find the GCF of* 24 *and* 18*. GCF* $= 6$*.*

2. *Divide each number by* 6*:* $24 \div 6 = 4$ *and* $18 \div 6 = 3$.
3. *Write:* $24 + 18 = 6(4 + 3)$.

Answer: $24 + 18 = 6(4 + 3) = 6 \times 7 = 42$

> *"Think of the distributive property like un-dealing cards. If every group got the same base amount, you can write it once on the outside!"*

Spot the Error

Mia wrote: $20 + 15 = 5(4 + 5)$.

What went wrong? $15 \div 5 = 3$, *not* 5. *The correct answer is* $5(4 + 3)$.

Distributive Property Practice

Rewrite Using the Distributive Property

1. $16 + 28 =$ ________________

2. $45 + 30 =$ ________________

3. $21 + 35 =$ ________________

4. $54 + 36 =$ ________________

Mental Math

5. *Use the distributive property to find 6×53 in your head.*

6. *A store sells shirts for \$12 each. You buy 8 shirts. Use the distributive property to find the total.*

★ 2.6 Understanding Positive and Negative Numbers ★

Learning Goals

- *Understand that positive and negative numbers show opposite directions*
- *Use positive and negative numbers in real-life contexts*
- *Identify what zero means in different situations*

Positive, Negative, and Zero

*Numbers go in **two directions** from zero:*

- ***Positive numbers** (+) are greater than zero:* $1, 2, 3, \ldots$
- ***Negative numbers** (−) are less than zero:* $-1, -2, -3, \ldots$
- ***Zero** is neither positive nor negative.*

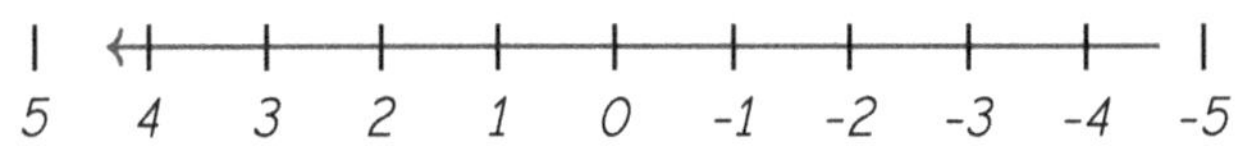

*Negative numbers are to the **left** of zero. Positive numbers are to the **right**.*

Where Do You See Negative Numbers?

- ***Temperature:*** $-10°F$ *means* 10 *degrees below zero.*
- ***Money:*** $-\$25$ *means you owe* $\$25$.
- ***Elevation:*** -50 *feet means* 50 *feet below sea level.*
- ***Football:*** *A* -7 *yard play means the team lost* 7 *yards.*

*In each case, **zero is the starting point**: $0°$, no debt, sea level, or the line of scrimmage.*

> *Zero is not "nothing" — it is the **boundary** between positive and negative!*

Positive and Negative Numbers Practice

Write the Number

1. A submarine is 200 feet below sea level. Write this as an integer.
2. A mountain peak is $3{,}400$ feet above sea level. Write this as an integer.
3. The temperature dropped 8 degrees below zero. Write the temperature.

What Does Zero Mean?

4. A bank account shows $\$0$. What does zero mean here?
5. On a number line, -3 is to the left of 0. Is -3 greater or less than zero?
6. -5 is a larger number than 3 because 5 is bigger than 3. True ○ False ○

2.7 Opposites and Absolute Value

Learning Goals

- Find the opposite of any number
- Understand that absolute value is distance from zero
- Use absolute value in real-world contexts

Opposites

Two numbers are **opposites** if they are the same distance from zero but on different sides.

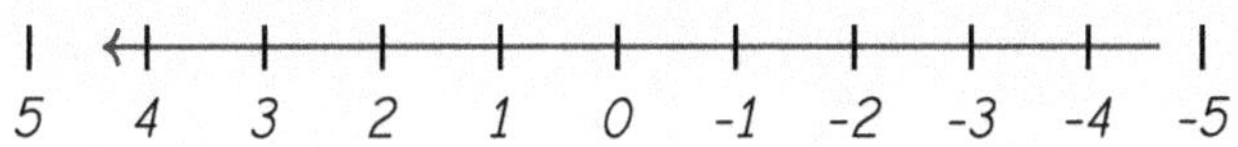

- The opposite of 4 is -4.
- The opposite of -3 is 3.
- The opposite of 0 is 0.

A number plus its opposite always equals zero: $5 + (-5) = 0$.

Absolute Value

The **absolute value** of a number is its distance from zero. Distance is always positive (or zero).

We write absolute value with bars: $|-7| = 7$ and $|7| = 7$.

Both -7 and 7 are 7 units from zero.

Absolute value strips away the sign. It only tells you "how far," not "which direction."

> *Think of absolute value as "How many steps to get back to zero?" Direction does not matter!*

Opposites and Absolute Value Practice

Find the Opposite

1. Opposite of 9

2. Opposite of -12

Find the Absolute Value

3. $|-15| =$

4. $|8| =$

Think Deeper

5. A diver is at -40 feet. A bird is at 25 feet. Who is farther from sea level?

6. $|-6| > |5|$ True ○ False ○

2.8 Rational Numbers on the Number Line

Learning Goals

- *Place integers, fractions, and decimals on a number line*
- *Explain placement using distance and direction from 0*
- *Understand that rational numbers include all of these forms*

A rational number is any number that can be written as a fraction $\frac{a}{b}$ where $b \neq 0$. This includes integers, fractions, and decimals.

Placing Numbers on the Number Line

Every rational number has an exact spot on the number line.

Steps:

1. *Decide the sign: positive (right of 0) or negative (left of 0).*
2. *Find the whole number part to know which two integers it falls between.*
3. *Use the fraction or decimal part to find the exact spot.*

-1.5 ***is halfway between*** -2 ***and*** -1. ***It is*** 1.5 ***units to the left of*** 0.

Plot $-\frac{3}{4}$ on a Number Line

Solution:

1. *Negative → left of zero.*
2. $\frac{3}{4}$ *is between* 0 *and* 1, *so* $-\frac{3}{4}$ *is between* -1 *and* 0.
3. *Divide the space from* -1 *to* 0 *into* 4 *equal parts. Go* 3 *parts from* 0.

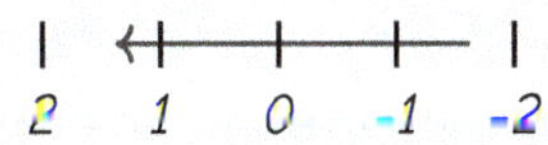

$-\frac{3}{4}$ *is* $\frac{3}{4}$ *of a unit to the left of zero.*

> **TIP**
> *Convert fractions to decimals if it helps:* $-\frac{3}{4} = -0.75$. *Then place it on the number line.*

Number Line Practice

Place on a Number Line

1. Where does $\frac{1}{2}$ go on a number line? Between which two integers?
2. Where does -2.25 go? Between which two integers?
3. Place $-\frac{5}{3}$ on a number line. Between which two integers?

Order and Compare

4. Which is farther from 0: -3.5 or 2.8?
5. List these in order from least to greatest: $\frac{1}{4}$, -1, 0.75, $-\frac{1}{2}$
6. -0.5 and $-\frac{1}{2}$ are the same point on the number line. True ◯ False ◯

2.9 The Coordinate Plane

Learning Goals

- *Plot points with positive and negative coordinates*
- *Identify the four quadrants*
- *Describe how changing signs reflects points across axes*

The Four Quadrants

A coordinate plane has two axes that cross at the **origin** $(0, 0)$. *They divide the plane into four quadrants:*

Quadrant	Signs of (x, y)	Example
I	$(+, +)$	$(3, 4)$
II	$(-, +)$	$(-2, 5)$
III	$(-, -)$	$(-1, -3)$
IV	$(+, -)$	$(4, -2)$

The first number (x) tells left/right. The second number (y) tells up/down.

Plot and Reflect

Plot $A = (3, 2)$. *Then plot its reflection across the* y*-axis.*

Solution:

1. *Start at the origin. Move* 3 *right and* 2 *up. That is* $A = (3, 2)$.

2. *To reflect across the y-axis, flip the x-coordinate sign.*
3. *The reflection is $(-3, 2)$.*

Answer: *The reflection of $(3, 2)$ across the y-axis is $(-3, 2)$.*

> *Reflecting across the y-axis changes the sign of x. Reflecting across the x-axis changes the sign of y. The other coordinate stays the same!*

Coordinate Plane Practice

Name the Quadrant

1. $(5, -3)$ is in Quadrant _____

2. $(-4, 7)$ is in Quadrant _____

Reflections

3. What is the reflection of $(2, -5)$ across the x-axis?

4. What is the reflection of $(-6, 1)$ across the y-axis?

Think Deeper

5. A point starts at $(-3, 4)$. It is reflected across the x-axis, then across the y-axis. Where does it end up?

6. The point $(0, -4)$ is on the y-axis. True ○ False ○

2.10 Comparing and Ordering Rational Numbers

Learning Goals

- *Compare rational numbers using $<$, $>$, and $=$*
- *Order rational numbers from least to greatest*
- *Explain comparisons in real world contexts*

Comparing on the Number Line

*On a number line, numbers get **larger** as you move right.*

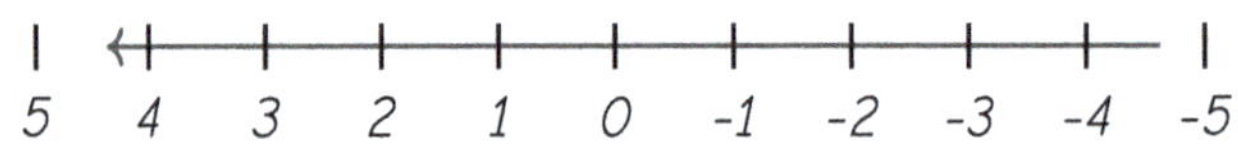

- *-3 is to the left of 1, so $-3 < 1$.*
- *-1 is to the right of -4, so $-1 > -4$.*

With negative numbers, the one closer to zero is greater.** $-2 > -7$ **because** -2 **is closer to zero.

Order a Mixed Set

Order from least to greatest: $-1.5,\ \frac{3}{4},\ -3,\ 0,\ 2.1$

Solution:

1. *Convert to decimals for easy comparison:* $-1.5, 0.75, -3, 0, 2.1$.
2. *Plot mentally on a number line, left to right.*

3. *Order:* $-3 < -1.5 < 0 < 0.75 < 2.1$.

Answer: $-3, \quad -1.5, \quad 0, \quad \frac{3}{4}, \quad 2.1$

TIP

Don't confuse number order with absolute value! $-8 < 3$ *as a number, but* $|-8| = 8 > |3| = 3$ *in absolute value.*

"When comparing negatives, think about a thermometer. $-5°$ *is colder (smaller) than* $-2°$ *even though* 5 *looks bigger!"*

Comparing and Ordering Practice

Compare: Write $<$, $>$, or $=$

1. -7 ______ -3
2. 0 ______ -6
3. -2.5 ______ -2.5
4. $\frac{1}{3}$ ______ $-\frac{1}{2}$

Order and Explain

5. *Order from least to greatest:* $5, -8, 3, -1, 0$
6. *The temperature on Monday was* $-4°C$*. On Tuesday it was* $-9°C$*. Which day was colder?*

★ 2.11 Distance on the Coordinate Plane ★

Learning Goals

- Find horizontal and vertical distances between points
- Use absolute value to compute distance
- Apply distance to real-world grid problems

Distance = Absolute Value of the Difference

When two points share the same x or the same y, you can find the distance between them:

Same x (vertical distance): Subtract the y-values and take the absolute value.

$$\text{Distance} = |y_1 - y_2|$$

Same y (horizontal distance): Subtract the x-values and take the absolute value.

$$\text{Distance} = |x_1 - x_2|$$

Absolute value makes sure the distance is always positive — you can't walk a negative number of steps!

Find the Distance

Vertical:

Find the distance between $(3, -2)$ *and* $(3, 5)$.

Both have $x = 3$. *Subtract* y*-values:* $|-2 - 5| = |-7| = 7$ *units.*

Horizontal:

Find the distance between $(-4, 1)$ *and* $(2, 1)$.

Both have $y = 1$. *Subtract* x*-values:* $|-4 - 2| = |-6| = 6$ *units.*

Distance Practice

Find the Distance

1. Distance between $(1, 4)$ and $(1, -3)$
2. Distance between $(-5, 2)$ and $(3, 2)$
3. Distance between $(0, -6)$ and $(0, 4)$
4. Distance between $(-3, -1)$ and $(-3, -9)$

Word Problems

5. A map grid shows a school at $(2, 5)$ and a library at $(2, -3)$. Each unit is 1 block. How many blocks apart are they?
6. Two traffic lights are at $(-7, 4)$ and $(5, 4)$. How far apart are they?

CHAPTER

3

Expressions and Equations

What's Inside

3.1	Exponents and Order of Operations	90
3.2	Translating Words into Expressions	93
3.3	Terms, Factors, and Coefficients	96
3.4	Evaluating Expressions	99
3.5	Equivalent Expressions	102
3.6	Variables in Real-World Problems	105
3.7	Solving One-Step Equations	108
3.8	Writing Inequalities	111
3.9	Graphing Inequalities on a Number Line	114
3.10	Two Quantities That Change Together	116

3.1 Exponents and Order of Operations

Learning Goals

- *Write repeated multiplication using exponents*
- *Evaluate expressions with whole-number exponents*
- *Apply the order of operations (PEMDAS)*

Exponents

*An **exponent** tells you how many times to multiply the base by itself.*

$3^4 = 3 \times 3 \times 3 \times 3 = 81$

- 3 *is the **base** — the number being multiplied.*
- 4 *is the **exponent** — how many times.*
- *We say "3 to the fourth power."*

Any number to the power of** 1 **is itself:** $7^1 = 7$**. Any number to the power of** 0 **is** 1**:** $5^0 = 1$**.

Order of Operations (PEMDAS)

Evaluate: $5 + 2 \times 3^2$

Solution:

1. *Exponents first:* $3^2 = 9$.
2. *Multiply:* $2 \times 9 = 18$.

3. *Add:* $5 + 18 = 23$.

Answer: 23

PEMDAS: Parentheses, Exponents, Multiply/Divide (left to right), Add/Subtract (left to right).

Exponents and Order of Operations Practice

Write Using Exponents

1. $7 \times 7 \times 7$

2. $2 \times 2 \times 2 \times 2 \times 2$

Evaluate

3. 4^3

4. $10^2 - 6 \times 5$

Apply PEMDAS

5. $(8 + 2)^2 \div 5$

6. *Maria says* $3 + 4 \times 2 = 14$*. Jake says the answer is* 11*. Who is correct?*

3.2 Translating Words into Expressions

Learning Goals

- Match math operations to everyday words
- Write algebraic expressions from word phrases
- Understand that order matters for subtraction and division

Words to Math

A **variable** is a letter that stands for a number. You can turn word phrases into math using a variable.

Word Phrase	Expression
A number plus 5	$n+5$
7 less than a number	$n-7$
Twice a number	$2n$
A number divided by 3	$n \div 3$

"Less than" flips the order. "7 less than n" is $n-7$, not $7-n$.

Translate a Phrase

Write an expression for: "Subtract y from 5."

Solution:

1. "Subtract y" means take y away.

2. "From 5" means start with 5.
3. Expression: $5 - y$.

Answer: $5 - y$

TIP

Read the phrase carefully. "5 from y" means $y - 5$. "y from 5" means $5 - y$. The number after "from" comes first.

Translating Words Practice

Write an Expression

1. The sum of 8 and a number k
2. 4 less than a number m
3. Triple a number w, then add 10
4. A number p divided by 6

Match Phrase to Expression

5. Which expression matches "9 more than twice x"?
6.

   A. $2x - 9$ B. $9 + 2x$ C. $9 \times 2x$ D. $2(x + 9)$

7. "Divide 10 by n" and "divide n by 10" give the same expression. True ○ False ○

3.3 Terms, Factors, and Coefficients

Learning Goals

- *Identify parts of an expression: terms, factors, coefficients, constants*
- *Recognize that a group like $(x + 7)$ can act as a single piece*

Parts of an Expression

An expression is made of ***terms*** *separated by $+$ or $-$ signs.*

Look at $3x + 5y - 2$:

- ***Terms****: $3x$, $5y$, and 2. Each chunk is one term.*
- ***Coefficient****: The number in front of a variable. In $3x$, the coefficient is 3.*
- ***Constant****: A term with no variable. Here it is 2.*
- ***Factors****: The pieces multiplied inside a term. In $3x$, the factors are 3 and x.*

If you see $2(x + 7)$, the two factors are 2 and $(x + 7)$. The group $(x + 7)$ counts as one factor.

Identify the Parts

Name the terms, coefficients, and constants in $4a + 9 - b$.

Solution:

1. *Terms: $4a$, 9, b.*
2. *Coefficients: 4 (for a) and 1 (for b, since $b = 1 \cdot b$).*

3. *Constant:* 9.

> “*When a variable has no number in front, its coefficient is* 1. *We just don't write it!*”

Terms, Factors, and Coefficients Practice

Identify the Parts

1. How many terms are in $7m + 3n - 5$?
2. What is the coefficient of y in $y + 12$?
3. Name the constant in $6k - 8 + 2k$.
4. In the expression $5(x + 3)$, what are the two factors?

True or False

5. In $9x$, the factors are 9 and x. True ○ False ○

6. The expression $4 + 2y$ has two constants. True ○ False ○

3.4 Evaluating Expressions

Learning Goals

- Substitute a number for a variable
- Use the order of operations to compute the value
- Evaluate expressions from real formulas

How to Evaluate

Evaluating means replacing each variable with a number and calculating.

Evaluate $3x + 7$ when $x = 4$:

1. Replace x with 4: $3(4) + 7$
2. Multiply: $12 + 7$
3. Add: 19

Always use parentheses when you substitute. Write $3(4)$, not 34.

Two Variables

Evaluate $2a - b^2$ when $a = 10$ and $b = 3$.

Solution:

1. Substitute: $2(10) - (3)^2$.
2. Exponent: $3^2 = 9$.

3. *Multiply:* $2(10) = 20$.

4. *Subtract:* $20 - 9 = 11$.

Answer: 11

TIP
Follow PEMDAS after you substitute. Exponents come before multiplication and addition.

Evaluating Expressions Practice

Evaluate

1. $5n - 3$ *when* $n = 6$

2. $x^2 + 4$ *when* $x = 5$

3. $\dfrac{a+b}{2}$ *when* $a = 8$, $b = 12$

4. $3(m - 4)$ *when* $m = 9$

Real-World Formulas

5. *The perimeter of a rectangle is* $P = 2l + 2w$. *Find* P *when* $l = 12$ *cm and* $w = 5$ *cm.*

6. *A phone plan costs* $\$20 + \$0.10 \times t$ *where* t *is the number of texts. Find the cost for* 150 *texts.*

★ 3.5 Equivalent Expressions ★

Learning Goals

- Use the distributive property to rewrite expressions
- Combine like terms
- Check equivalence by substituting values

Equivalent Expressions

Two expressions are **equivalent** if they give the same value for every number.

The Distributive Property

$a(b+c) = ab + ac$

$3(x+4) = 3x + 12$

Combining Like Terms

Like terms have the same variable. Add their coefficients.

$5n + 3 + 2n = 7n + 3$

You can check: plug in $n = 2$. Left: $5(2) + 3 + 2(2) = 17$. Right: $7(2) + 3 = 17$. Same!

Simplify an Expression

Simplify: $4(x+5) + 3x$

Solution:

1. *Distribute:* $4x + 20 + 3x$.
2. *Combine like terms:* $4x + 3x = 7x$.
3. *Result:* $7x + 20$.

Answer: $7x + 20$

Think of like terms as matching groups. $5n$ and $2n$ are both "n-groups," so you can put them together: $7n$.

Equivalent Expressions Practice

Simplify

1. $6x + 2x - 4$

2. $2(y + 9)$

3. $3(2m + 1) + 5m$

Equivalence Check

4. *Are* $4(n + 2)$ *and* $4n + 8$ *equivalent? Test with* $n = 3$.

5. $3x + 5x = 8x^2$ *True* ○ *False* ○

6. *Write an equivalent expression for* $10a - 2a + 7$.

★ 3.6 Variables in Real-World Problems ★

Learning Goals

- *Use variables to describe unknown or changing quantities*
- *Write expressions and equations from real situations*
- *Understand that a variable can stand for one value or many*

Variables Represent Real Quantities

*A **variable** is a letter that stands for a number you don't know yet.*

One unknown value: *A skateboard costs $\$45$ and you have d dollars. After buying it you have $d - 45$ dollars left. Here d is one specific amount — whatever is in your wallet.*

Any value in a set: *A square has side length s. Its perimeter is $4s$. Here s could be any positive number — the formula works for all of them.*

Always say what the variable means. "Let h = number of hours" keeps your work clear.

Write an Expression from a Story

A movie ticket costs $\$12$ per person. Your group also pays $\$6$ for popcorn. Write an expression for the total cost when p people go.

Solution:

1. *Tickets:* $12 \times p = 12p$.
2. *Popcorn (one-time):* 6.
3. *Total:* $12p + 6$.

Answer: $12p + 6$

TIP

*Look for what **changes** and what **stays the same**. The changing part gets a variable. The fixed part is a number.*

Variables in Real-World Problems Practice

Write an Expression

1. A gym charges $\$25$ to join and $\$10$ per month. Write an expression for the total cost after m months.
2. You have 50 songs and download n more each week. Write an expression for the total after w weeks.
3. A rectangle has length l and width 3. Write an expression for its area.

Choose the Variable

4. A pizza costs $\$14$. You split it equally among friends. What variable do you need, and what is each person's share?
5. In $P = 4s$, the variable s can only be one number. True ○ False ○

3.7 Solving One-Step Equations

Learning Goals

- Solve equations of the form $x + p = q$ and $px = q$
- Use inverse operations to isolate the variable
- Check solutions by substituting back

Solving with Inverse Operations

An **equation** says two sides are equal. To solve, undo the operation to get the variable alone.

Addition $\rightarrow$ Subtract

$x + 8 = 15$

Subtract 8 from both sides: $x = 15 - 8 = 7$.

Multiplication $\rightarrow$ Divide

$4x = 36$

Divide both sides by 4: $x = 36 \div 4 = 9$.

Whatever you do to one side, you must do to the other side.

Solve and Check

Solve $x - 5 = 12$.

Solution:

1. *Subtraction is the operation. Undo it by adding* 5.
2. $x = 12 + 5 = 17$.
3. *Check:* $17 - 5 = 12$. ✓

Answer: $x = 17$

> *Always check your answer. Plug it back into the original equation. Both sides should match!*

Solving One-Step Equations Practice

Solve Each Equation

1. $y + 9 = 20$
2. $m - 7 = 15$
3. $6k = 54$
4. $\dfrac{n}{5} = 8$

Word Problems

5. *A book costs $\$7$ more than a magazine. The book costs $\$19$. Write and solve an equation for the magazine price m.*

6. *Three friends split a bill equally and each paid $\$14$. Write and solve an equation for the total bill b.*

★ 3.8 Writing Inequalities ★

Learning Goals

- *Write inequalities using $<, >, \leq, \geq$*
- *Translate phrases like "at least" and "no more than"*
- *Understand that inequalities have many solutions*

Inequality Symbols

*An **inequality** compares two values that may not be equal.*

Symbol	Meaning	Phrase
$<$	less than	"fewer than," "under"
$>$	greater than	"more than," "over"
$\leq$	less than or equal to	"at most," "no more than"
$\geq$	greater than or equal to	"at least," "no fewer than"

***"At least 5" means 5 or more:** $x \geq 5$. **"At most 5" means 5 or fewer:** $x \leq 5$.*

Turn Words into an Inequality

A roller coaster requires riders to be at least 48 inches tall. Write an inequality for the height h.

Solution:

1. *"At least 48" means 48 or more.*

2. *Use* $\geq$*:* $h \geq 48$.

Answer: $h \geq 48$

"At least" and "no fewer than" both mean $\geq$. "At most" and "no more than" both mean $\leq$.

Writing Inequalities Practice

Write an Inequality

1. You must be under 13 to get the kids' price. Let a = age.
2. A bag can hold at most 50 pounds. Let w = weight.
3. You need at least \$20 to buy the game. Let d = dollars you have.
4. The temperature stayed below 0 degrees. Let t = temperature.

Think Deeper

5. Is $x = 5$ a solution to $x > 5$?
6. The inequality $n \leq 10$ has exactly 10 solutions. True ○ False ○

3.9 Graphing Inequalities on a Number Line

Learning Goals

- *Graph inequalities on a number line*
- *Use open and closed circles correctly*
- *Test values to check if they are solutions*

How to Graph an Inequality

Draw a number line. Mark the boundary number. Then shade the direction that makes the inequality true.

- ***Open circle*** ○*: the number is NOT included* ($<$ *or* $>$*).*
- ***Closed circle*** ●*: the number IS included* ($\leq$ *or* $\geq$*).*

Example: $x > 3$ → *open circle at* 3*, shade right.*

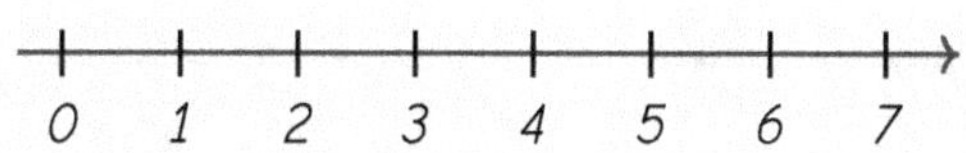

Example: $x \leq 5$ → *closed circle at* 5*, shade left.*

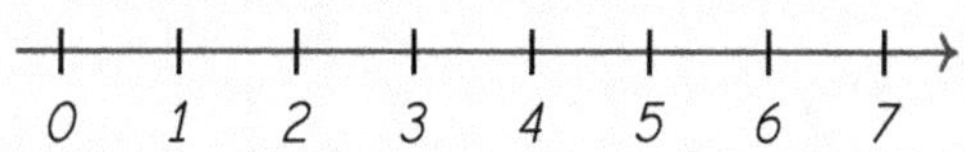

> TIP
> *To check your graph, pick a number in the shaded region and plug it in. If it makes the inequality true, you shaded the right way.*

Graphing Inequalities Practice

Describe the Graph

1. $x \geq 2$: *Open or closed circle at 2? Shade left or right?*
2. $x < 7$: *Open or closed circle at 7? Shade left or right?*

Test a Value

3. *Is* $x = 4$ *a solution to* $x \leq 4$?
4. *Is* $x = -1$ *a solution to* $x > 0$?

Write and Graph

5. *A pool opens when the temperature is more than* $75°$*F. Write an inequality for* t *and describe the graph.*
6. *Write an inequality whose graph has a closed circle at* -3 *and shades to the left.*

★ 3.10 Two Quantities That Change Together ★

Learning Goals

- *Identify independent and dependent variables*
- *Represent relationships with tables, equations, and graphs*
- *Describe how one quantity depends on another*

Independent and Dependent Variables

When two quantities change together, one **controls** *and the other* **responds**.

Example: *You earn \$8 per hour. The more hours you work, the more money you earn.*

- **Independent variable**: *hours* (h) *— you choose this.*
- **Dependent variable**: *earnings* (e) *— this depends on hours.*
- **Equation**: $e = 8h$.

Hours and Earnings

h (hours)	1	2	3	4	5
e (dollars)	8	16	24	32	40

The independent variable goes on the x-axis. The dependent variable goes on the y-axis.

Identify and Write an Equation

A plant grows 2 cm each week. Write an equation and make a table for the first 4 weeks.

Solution:

1. *Independent: weeks (w). Dependent: height (h).*
2. *Equation: $h = 2w$.*
3. *Table: $w = 1 \to h = 2$; $w = 2 \to 4$; $w = 3 \to 6$; $w = 4 \to 8$.*

TIP

Ask yourself: "Which one do I pick, and which one follows?" The one you pick is independent.

Two Quantities Practice

Identify the Variables

1. A car travels 60 miles per hour. Name the independent and dependent variables.
2. A phone battery loses 5% each hour. Name the independent and dependent variables.

Write and Use Equations

3. A pizza shop charges \$10 per pizza. Write an equation for the cost c of p pizzas. Find the cost of 7 pizzas.
4. The equation $d = 3t$ shows how far a turtle walks. Complete: when $t = 5$, $d =$ ____________.
5. In $y = x + 4$, the variable x is the dependent variable. True ○ False ○

CHAPTER

4

Geometry: Area, Surface Area, and Volume

What's Inside

4.1 Area of Triangles 120

4.2 Area of Parallelograms and Trapezoids 123

4.3 Volume of Rectangular Prisms 126

4.4 Polygons on the Coordinate Plane 129

4.5 Finding Area on the Coordinate Plane 132

4.6 Nets and Surface Area 135

4.1 Area of Triangles

Learning Goals

- *Find the area of a triangle using the formula*
- *Connect triangle area to rectangle area*
- *Identify the base and height of a triangle*

Triangle Area

Every triangle is half of a rectangle.

Area of a Triangle

$$A = \frac{1}{2} \times b \times h$$

- b = **base** — *any side of the triangle.*
- h = **height** — *the perpendicular distance from the base to the opposite vertex.*

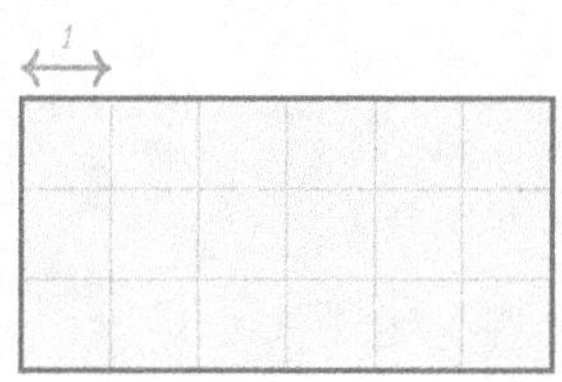

A 6×3 rectangle has area 18. A triangle with the same base and height has area $18 \div 2 = 9$.

The height must be perpendicular (at a right angle) to the base. It is NOT always a side of the triangle.

Find the Area

A triangle has base 10 cm and height 7 cm. Find its area.

Solution:

1. $A = \frac{1}{2} \times 10 \times 7$
2. $A = \frac{1}{2} \times 70 = 35$

Answer: $A = 35$ cm^2

TIP

Multiply the base and height first, then divide by 2. It's easier than multiplying by $\frac{1}{2}$ first.

Area of Triangles Practice

Find the Area

1. Base $= 8$ in, height $= 5$ in.
2. Base $= 12$ cm, height $= 9$ cm.
3. Base $= 3.5$ m, height $= 4$ m.
4. Base $= 6$ ft, height $= 6$ ft.

Apply It

5. A triangular sail has a base of 4 m and a height of 6 m. How much fabric is needed?
6. A triangle with base 10 and height 4 has the same area as one with base 8 and height 5. **True** ○ **False** ○

4.2 Area of Parallelograms and Trapezoids

Learning Goals

- Find the area of parallelograms using base and height
- Find the area of trapezoids using the formula
- Decompose shapes to find area

Area Formulas

Parallelogram

A parallelogram can be cut and rearranged into a rectangle.

$A = b \times h$

*The **height** is perpendicular to the base — it is NOT the slanted side.*

Trapezoid

*A trapezoid has two parallel sides called **bases** (b_1 and b_2).*

$A = \frac{1}{2} \times (b_1 + b_2) \times h$

Add the two bases, multiply by the height, then take half.

Find Each Area

Parallelogram

Base $= 9$ *cm, height* $= 4$ *cm.*

$A = 9 \times 4 = 36$ cm^2.

Trapezoid

$b_1 = 5$ *in*, $b_2 = 11$ *in*, $h = 6$ *in*.

$A = \frac{1}{2} \times (5 + 11) \times 6 = \frac{1}{2} \times 16 \times 6 = 48$ *in*^{2}.

> *"For a parallelogram, the slanted side is NOT the height. Look for the line that makes a right angle with the base."*

Area Practice

Parallelograms

1. Base $= 7$ m, height $= 3$ m.

2. Base $= 10$ ft, height $= 5.5$ ft.

Trapezoids

3. $b_1 = 4$ cm, $b_2 = 8$ cm, $h = 5$ cm.

4. $b_1 = 3$ in, $b_2 = 9$ in, $h = 4$ in.

Apply It

5. A park is shaped like a trapezoid with parallel sides 40 m and 60 m, and height 30 m. What is the area?

6. A parallelogram with base 6 and height 4 has the same area as a rectangle that is 6 by 4. **True** ○ **False** ○

4.3 Volume of Rectangular Prisms

Learning Goals

- *Find the volume of rectangular prisms using $V = lwh$*
- *Work with fractional edge lengths*
- *Interpret volume as unit cubes that fit inside*

Volume of a Rectangular Prism

Volume measures how much space a 3D shape fills. For a rectangular prism (a box):

Volume

$$V = l \times w \times h$$

- l = length, w = width, h = height.
- Volume is measured in **cubic units** (cm^3, in^3, ft^3).
- Think of it as: how many unit cubes fit inside the box?

You can also find volume in two steps: area of the base $\times$ height. The base is a rectangle, so its area is $l \times w$.

Fractional Edge Lengths

A box is $2\frac{1}{2}$ ft long, 4 ft wide, and 3 ft tall. Find the volume.

Solution:

1. *Convert:* $2\frac{1}{2} = 2.5$.
2. $V = 2.5 \times 4 \times 3$.
3. $2.5 \times 4 = 10$. *Then* $10 \times 3 = 30$.

Answer: $V = 30$ *ft*^{3}

TIP

When edges are fractions, convert to decimals or improper fractions first. Then multiply step by step.

Volume Practice

Find the Volume

1. $l = 6$ cm, $w = 4$ cm, $h = 5$ cm.
2. $l = 8$ in, $w = 3$ in, $h = 2$ in.
3. $l = 1.5$ m, $w = 2$ m, $h = 4$ m.
4. $l = \frac{1}{2}$ ft, $w = \frac{1}{2}$ ft, $h = \frac{1}{2}$ ft.

Apply It

5. A fish tank is 20 in long, 10 in wide, and 12 in tall. What is its volume?
6. A box has volume 60 cm^3. Its length is 5 cm and width is 4 cm. What is the height?

★ 4.4 Polygons on the Coordinate Plane ★

Learning Goals

- *Plot vertices to draw polygons on the coordinate plane*
- *Find lengths of horizontal and vertical sides using coordinates*
- *Use absolute value to calculate side lengths*

Drawing Shapes with Coordinates

*You can draw a polygon by plotting its **vertices** (corners) and connecting them.*

***Horizontal sides** have the same y-coordinate. Their length is the distance between the x-values.*

***Vertical sides** have the same x-coordinate. Their length is the distance between the y-values.*

***Example:** Points $(2, 3)$ and $(2, -1)$ form a vertical side.*

Length $= |3 - (-1)| = |4| = 4$ *units.*

When coordinates cross zero, use absolute value: add the distances from each point to zero. $|3| + |-1| = 4.$

Find the Side Lengths

A rectangle has vertices $A(-3, 2)$, $B(5, 2)$, $C(5, -1)$, $D(-3, -1)$. *Find the length and width.*

Solution:

1. *Side* AB *is horizontal* ($y = 2$). *Length* $= |5 - (-3)| = 8$ *units.*

2. *Side BC is vertical ($x = 5$). Length $= |2 - (-1)| = 3$ units.*

Answer: Length $=$ 8 units, width $=$ 3 units.

> *Same $y \to$ horizontal side (subtract x-values). Same $x \to$ vertical side (subtract y-values). Always use absolute value!*

Polygons on the Coordinate Plane Practice

Find the Side Length

1. Points $(1,4)$ and $(1,-2)$. What is the distance?
2. Points $(-5,3)$ and $(3,3)$. What is the distance?

Plot and Measure

3. A triangle has vertices $(0,0)$, $(6,0)$, $(3,4)$. What is the length of the base along the x-axis?
4. A square has vertices $(2,2)$, $(2,-2)$, $(-2,-2)$, $(-2,2)$. What is the side length?

Challenge

5. A rectangle has vertices $(-4,5)$, $(6,5)$, $(6,-3)$, $(-4,-3)$. Find the perimeter.

4.5 Finding Area on the Coordinate Plane

Learning Goals

- *Find side lengths of polygons using coordinates*
- *Calculate the area of rectangles and triangles on the coordinate plane*
- *Break irregular shapes into simpler pieces to find area*

Area from Coordinates

Once you know the side lengths from coordinates, use your area formulas:

- **Rectangle:** $A = l \times w$
- **Triangle:** $A = \frac{1}{2} \times b \times h$ *(use horizontal base and vertical height)*

For ***irregular shapes****, break them into rectangles and triangles you know how to measure. Then add the areas together.*

Area of a Rectangle on the Plane

A rectangle has vertices $(-2, 1)$, $(4, 1)$, $(4, -3)$, $(-2, -3)$. *Find the area.*

Solution:

1. *Length (horizontal):* $|4 - (-2)| = 6$ *units.*
2. *Width (vertical):* $|1 - (-3)| = 4$ *units.*
3. *Area* $= 6 \times 4 = 24$ *sq units.*

Answer: 24 **square units**

TIP

I

f a shape is hard to measure directly, draw a rectangle around it and subtract the parts you don't need!

Finding Area on the Coordinate Plane Practice

Find the Area

1. *A rectangle has vertices* $(0,0)$, $(5,0)$, $(5,3)$, $(0,3)$. *Find the area.*
2. *A rectangle has vertices* $(-3,4)$, $(3,4)$, $(3,-2)$, $(-3,-2)$. *Find the area.*
3. *A right triangle has vertices* $(0,0)$, $(8,0)$, $(0,6)$. *Find the area.*
4. *A right triangle has vertices* $(1,1)$, $(1,7)$, $(5,1)$. *Find the area.*

Challenge

5. *An L-shaped figure has vertices* $(0,0)$, $(6,0)$, $(6,2)$, $(3,2)$, $(3,5)$, $(0,5)$. *Split it into two rectangles and find the total area.*

4.6 Nets and Surface Area

Learning Goals

- *Identify nets of 3D shapes (rectangular prisms, triangular prisms, pyramids)*
- *Find surface area by adding the areas of all faces*
- *Solve real-world problems involving surface area*

What Is a Net?

*A **net** is a flat pattern that folds into a 3D shape. Each part of the net becomes one **face** of the solid.*

***Surface area** is the total area of all the faces of a 3D shape.*

Rectangular Prism (6 faces)

A rectangular prism has 3 pairs of matching faces: SA $= 2lw + 2lh + 2wh$

Triangular Prism (5 faces)

2 triangular bases + 3 rectangular sides.

Think of wrapping a gift box—surface area is how much wrapping paper you need!

Surface Area of a Rectangular Prism

Find the surface area of a box that is 5 *cm long,* 3 *cm wide, and* 4 *cm tall.*

Solution:

1. $SA = 2lw + 2lh + 2wh$
2. $= 2(5)(3) + 2(5)(4) + 2(3)(4)$
3. $= 30 + 40 + 24 = 94$

Answer: 94 cm^2

"*Always label your answer in **square units** (like cm^2 or in^2) because surface area measures flat space, not volume!*"

Nets and Surface Area Practice

Surface Area of Rectangular Prisms

1. Find the surface area: $l = 6$ in, $w = 4$ in, $h = 2$ in.
2. A cube has edges of 5 cm. Find the surface area.
3. Find the surface area: $l = 10$ m, $w = 3$ m, $h = 7$ m.

Real-World Problems

4. Maya paints all sides of a wooden crate measuring 2 ft by 3 ft by 4 ft. How many square feet does she paint?

Challenge

5. A triangular prism has two right triangle bases with legs 3 cm and 4 cm and hypotenuse 5 cm. The prism is 10 cm long. Find the total surface area.

CHAPTER

5

Statistics and Data

What's Inside

5.1 Statistical Questions 139

5.2 Describing Data: Center, Spread, and Shape 142

5.3 Mean and Median 145

5.4 Measures of Spread 148

5.5 Dot Plots and Histograms 151

5.6 Box Plots 154

5.7 Summarizing Data and Making Comparisons 157

★ 5.1 Statistical Questions ★

Learning Goals

- *Tell the difference between statistical and non-statistical questions*
- *Understand that statistical questions expect answers that vary*
- *Write your own statistical questions to collect data*

What Makes a Question Statistical?

*A **statistical question** is one where you expect* different *answers from different people or situations.*

Statistical

"How many hours do sixth graders sleep each night?"

*Different students sleep different amounts, so the answers **vary**.*

Not Statistical

"How many hours are in a day?"

*There is only one answer: 24. The answer does **not** vary.*

If the answer can change from person to person (or time to time), it's a statistical question.

"A quick test: ask yourself, "Would I get different answers if I asked 10 people?" If yes, it's statistical!"

Why Statistical Questions Matter

Scientists, coaches, and businesses all use statistical questions to collect data and make decisions. A coach might ask, "How many free throws does each player make out of 10?" The answers vary, and the coach uses the data to plan practice.

Statistical Questions Practice

Statistical or Not?

1. *"What is the capital of France?"*
2. *"How many pets do students in our class have?"*
3. *"How tall are the students in sixth grade?"*
4. *"What is 7×8?"*

Challenge

5. *Write a statistical question you could ask your classmates. Explain why the answers would vary.*

5.2 Describing Data: Center, Spread, and Shape

Learning Goals

- *Describe a data set using center, spread, and overall shape*
- *Identify clusters, gaps, peaks, and outliers*
- *Explain what these features tell us about the data*

Three Ways to Describe Data

When you look at a data set, ask three questions:

Center

Where is the "middle" of the data? This is a typical value. (You'll learn exact ways to find it in the next topic.)

Spread

How spread out are the values? Are they bunched close together or scattered far apart?

Shape

What does the data look like on a graph? Is it symmetric (even on both sides), skewed (stretched to one side), or does it have gaps?

Describing a Data Set

Test scores: $72, 78, 80, 81, 82, 83, 85, 95$.

Solution:

1. ***Center:*** *Most scores are around* 80–83.

2. ***Spread:*** *Scores range from 72 to 95 (range $= 23$).*

3. ***Shape:*** *Most values cluster in the 78–85 range. The 95 is an* ***outlier*** *(far from the rest). The 72 is also a bit separated—a small* ***gap****.*

> *An* ***outlier*** *is a value that is much higher or lower than the rest. It can pull the center away from the typical values!*

Describing Data Practice

Identify the Feature

1. *Data:* $10, 11, 12, 12, 13, 13, 14$. *Is this data set spread out or bunched together?*

2. *Data:* $3, 5, 6, 7, 7, 8, 25$. *Is there an outlier? If so, which value?*

3. *Data:* $20, 22, 23, 23, 24, 24, 24, 25, 26$. *Where is the center of this data?*

Challenge

4. *Two students measured how many pages they read each day for a week. Student A:* $10, 12, 11, 13, 12, 11, 12$. *Student B:* $2, 5, 8, 12, 18, 22, 30$. *Which student's data is more spread out? Explain.*

5.3 Mean and Median

Learning Goals

- Calculate the mean (average) of a data set
- Find the median (middle value) of a data set
- Decide which measure of center is more useful

Two Ways to Find the Center

Mean (Average)

Add all the values, then divide by how many there are.

$$\text{Mean} = \frac{\text{sum of all values}}{\text{number of values}}$$

Median (Middle Value)

Put the values in order from least to greatest. The middle number is the median.

*If there are **two** middle numbers, find their average.*

Finding Mean and Median

Data: $4, 8, 6, 10, 7.$

Solution:

1. **Mean:** $4 + 8 + 6 + 10 + 7 = 35$. *Divide:* $35 \div 5 = 7$.
2. **Median:** *Order the data:* $4, 6, 7, 8, 10$. *The middle value is* 7.

Answer: *Mean* $= 7$, *Median* $= 7$

TIP

The mean is pulled toward outliers. If one value is very high or very low, the ***median*** *is a better measure of center.*

"*Even number of values? Average the two middle numbers! Example: middle values* 6 *and* $8 \rightarrow$ *median* $= \frac{6+8}{2} = 7$."

Mean and Median Practice

Find the Mean and Median

1. Data: $3, 5, 7, 9, 11$. Find the mean and median.
2. Data: $12, 15, 18, 20$. Find the mean and median.
3. Data: $2, 3, 4, 5, 100$. Find the mean. Is the mean a good description of a "typical" value? Why or why not?

Challenge

4. Five friends scored $80, 85, 90, 92, 88$ on a test. A sixth friend scored 40. How does adding this score change the mean?

5.4 Measures of Spread

Learning Goals

- *Find the range, interquartile range (IQR), and mean absolute deviation (MAD)*
- *Explain what each measure tells us about how spread out data is*
- *Compare data sets using measures of spread*

How Spread Out Is the Data?

Range

Range = greatest value − least value

Simple, but one outlier can make the range huge.

Interquartile Range (IQR)

The IQR measures the spread of the ***middle half*** *of the data.*

IQR $= Q3 - Q1$

$Q1$ *is the median of the lower half.* $Q3$ *is the median of the upper half.*

Mean Absolute Deviation (MAD)

The MAD tells you how far, on average, each value is from the mean.

Steps: (1) Find the mean. (2) Find each value's distance from the mean. (3) Average those distances.

Finding Range and IQR

Data (in order): $2, 4, 5, 7, 9, 12, 15.$

Solution:

1. ***Range:*** $15 - 2 = 13$.
2. ***Median:*** 7 *(the 4th value out of 7).*
3. $Q1$*: Median of* $2, 4, 5 = 4$. $Q3$*: Median of* $9, 12, 15 = 12$.
4. ***IQR:*** $12 - 4 = 8$.

Answer: ***Range*** $= 13$, ***IQR*** $= 8$

*“A **small** IQR or MAD means the data is consistent. A **large** one means the data is spread out!”*

Measures of Spread Practice

Find Range and IQR

1. *Data:* $10, 14, 18, 22, 26$. *Find the range.*
2. *Data:* $3, 5, 7, 8, 10, 12, 14$. *Find $Q1$, $Q3$, and the IQR.*

Mean Absolute Deviation

3. *Data:* $4, 6, 8, 10, 12$. *The mean is* 8. *Find the MAD.*
4. *Data:* $10, 10, 10, 10, 10$. *What is the MAD?*

Challenge

5. *Team A scores:* $50, 55, 60, 65, 70$. *Team B scores:* $20, 40, 60, 80, 100$. *Both have the same mean* (60). *Which team is more consistent? Use the range to explain.*

5.5 Dot Plots and Histograms

Learning Goals

- *Read and interpret dot plots*
- *Read and interpret histograms*
- *Choose when each type of display is most useful*

Two Ways to Display Data

Dot Plot

A dot plot places a dot above a number line for each data value. It shows ***every individual value****, so you can see clusters, gaps, and outliers easily.*

Best for: ***small data sets*** *where you want to see each value.*

Histogram

A histogram groups data into ***equal intervals*** *(called bins) and uses bars to show how many values fall in each interval.*

Best for: ***large data sets*** *where individual values would be hard to read.*

Dot plots show individual dots. Histogram bars show counts for a range of values—no gaps between bars!

Reading a Dot Plot

A dot plot shows quiz scores: two dots above 7, four dots above 8, three dots above 9, one dot above 10.

Solution:

1. *Total students:* $2 + 4 + 3 + 1 = 10$.
2. *Most common score (mode):* 8 *(it has the most dots).*
3. *Range:* $10 - 7 = 3$.

TIP

In a histogram, the height of each bar tells you how many values are in that interval. A taller bar means more data points in that range.

Dot Plots and Histograms Practice

Dot Plot Questions

1. *A dot plot of daily high temperatures shows: 68°F (1 dot), 70°F (3 dots), 72°F (4 dots), 74°F (2 dots). How many days of data are shown?*
2. *Using the same dot plot, what is the most common temperature?*

Histogram Questions

3. *A histogram shows test scores in bins: 60–69 (3 students), 70–79 (8 students), 80–89 (12 students), 90–100 (7 students). How many students scored 80 or above?*
4. *Which interval has the fewest students?*

Challenge

5. *Would you use a dot plot or a histogram to display the ages of 500 people at a concert? Explain.*

5.6 Box Plots

Learning Goals

- *Find the five-number summary of a data set*
- *Read and interpret box plots*
- *Compare two data sets using box plots*

The Five-Number Summary

A **box plot** (also called a box-and-whisker plot) displays five key values:

1. **Minimum** — the smallest value
2. $Q1$ (first quartile) — median of the lower half
3. **Median** $(Q2)$ — the middle value
4. $Q3$ (third quartile) — median of the upper half
5. **Maximum** — the largest value

The **box** stretches from $Q1$ to $Q3$. A line inside marks the median. The **whiskers** extend to the minimum and maximum.

The box contains the middle 50% **of the data. The IQR** $= Q3 - Q1$ **is the width of the box.**

Building a Five-Number Summary

Data (in order): $10, 14, 18, 22, 25, 30, 35.$

Solution:

1. **Min** $= 10$, **Max** $= 35$.
2. **Median:** 22 (the 4th value out of 7).
3. $Q1$: Median of $10, 14, 18 = 14$.
4. $Q3$: Median of $25, 30, 35 = 30$.

Answer: Five-number summary: $10, 14, 22, 30, 35$

"A longer box means more spread in the middle half. Compare boxes to see which group is more consistent!"

Box Plots Practice

Five-Number Summary

1. Data: $5, 8, 12, 15, 20, 24, 28$. Find the five-number summary.

2. Data: $2, 4, 6, 8, 10, 12$. Find the median and IQR.

Reading Box Plots

3. A box plot shows: min $= 40$, $Q1 = 55$, median $= 65$, $Q3 = 80$, max $= 95$. What percent of the data falls between 55 and 80?

4. Using the same box plot, what is the IQR?

Challenge

5. Class A box plot: median $= 75$, IQR $= 10$. Class B box plot: median $= 75$, IQR $= 30$. Both have the same median. Which class has more consistent scores?

5.7 Summarizing Data and Making Comparisons

Learning Goals

- *Summarize a data set using center and spread together*
- *Compare two data sets using numbers and graphs*
- *Support claims about data with evidence*

Putting It All Together

A good data summary uses ***both*** *center and spread:*

- ***Center*** *(mean or median) tells you what is typical.*
- ***Spread*** *(range, IQR, or MAD) tells you how consistent the data is.*

When ***comparing two groups****, ask:*

1. *Which group has a higher center?*
2. *Which group is more spread out?*
3. *Do the data sets overlap a lot or a little?*

Use the median and IQR when data is skewed or has outliers. Use the mean and MAD when data is roughly symmetric.

Comparing Two Teams

Team A test scores: mean $= 82$*, MAD* $= 3$*.* *Team B: mean* $= 78$*, MAD* $= 9$*.*

Solution:

1. ***Center:*** *Team A's mean (82) is higher than Team B's (78).*
2. ***Spread:*** *Team A's MAD is 3 (very consistent). Team B's MAD is 9 (more spread out).*
3. ***Conclusion:*** *Team A scored higher on average* and *was more consistent.*

"Always back up your claims with numbers! Don't just say "Group A did better." Say why: "Group A's median was 10 points higher.""

Summarizing Data Practice

Summarize the Data

1. *Data:* $15, 18, 20, 22, 25$. *Find the mean and range, then write one sentence summarizing the data.*

2. *Data:* $5, 5, 6, 6, 6, 7, 7, 50$. *Would you use the mean or median to describe a typical value? Explain.*

Compare Two Groups

3. *Class A: median* $= 85$*, IQR* $= 8$. *Class B: median* $= 80$*, IQR* $= 20$. *Which class performed better and more consistently?*

4. *Store A daily sales: mean* $= \$400$*, MAD* $= \$50$. *Store B: mean* $= \$400$*, MAD* $= \$150$. *The means are equal. What does the MAD tell you?*

Challenge

5. *A soccer team scored these goals per game:* $1, 2, 2, 3, 3, 3, 4$. *A basketball team scored:* $60, 65, 70, 75, 80, 85, 90$. *Jayden says the basketball team is "more spread out" because their range* (30) *is bigger than the soccer team's range* (3)*. Do you agree? Explain.*

Answer Key

★ Check Your Answers! ★

Try each problem first, then look here to check your work.
It's OK to make mistakes — that's how we learn ★

Chapter 1

Section 1.1

1. 6 *to* 10, $6:10$, $\frac{6}{10}$
2. 10 *to* 6, $10:6$, $\frac{10}{6}$
3. 6 *to* 16, $6:16$, $\frac{6}{16}$
4. $3:5$
5. $\frac{8}{14}$
6. $9:15$
7. 8 *tablets*
8. 9 *children*

Explanations

1. *Apples first, then oranges.*

2. *Oranges first, then apples.*

3. *Total* $= 6 + 10 = 16$. *This is a part-to-whole ratio.*

6. *Total games* $= 9 + 6 = 15$.

7. $20 \div 5 = 4$ *groups.* $4 \times 2 = 8$ *tablets.*

8 $21 \div 7 = 3$ groups. $3 \times 3 = 9$ children.

Section 1.2

1 $6:5$

2 $4:1$

3 $3:8$

4 $3:5$

5 15 boys

6 48 rows of corn

7 Answers will vary.

8 20 practice days and 4 game days

Explanations

4 Non-raisins $= 8 - 3 = 5$.

5 Total parts $= 3 + 5 = 8$. Each part $= 40 \div 8 = 5$. Boys $= 3 \times 5 = 15$.

6 Total parts $= 4 + 1 = 5$. Each part $= 60 \div 5 = 12$. Corn $= 4 \times 12 = 48$.

7 Example: For every 2 rainy days, there are 7 sunny days.

8 Total parts $= 5 + 1 = 6$. Each part $= 24 \div 6 = 4$. Practice $= 5 \times 4 = 20$. Games $= 1 \times 4 = 4$.

Section 1.3

1 Rate

2 Ratio

3 Rate

4 Ratio

5 $\frac{180 \text{ miles}}{3 \text{ hours}}$ or 180 miles per 3 hours

6 $\frac{500 \text{ toys}}{4 \text{ days}}$ or 500 toys per 4 days

7 The cyclist is faster.

8 Answers will vary.

Explanations

1 *Touchdowns and games are different units.*

2 *Both are shirts (same unit).*

3 *Calories and granola bars are different units.*

4 *Both describe people — this is part-to-whole.*

7 *Runner:* $12 \div 6 = 2$ *minutes per lap. Cyclist:* $8 \div 6 \approx 1.33$ *minutes per lap. The cyclist takes less time per lap.*

8 *Examples: miles per hour while driving, dollars per gallon of gas, songs per hour on a playlist.*

Section 1.4

1 *2 laps per minute*

2 *75 cans per hour*

3 *$12 per hour*

4 *600 miles per hour*

5 *The 12-pack*

6 *The 28 oz jar is the better deal.*

7 *30 miles per gallon*

8 *Ethan reads faster.*

Explanations

1 $20 \div 10 = 2$

2 $450 \div 6 = 75$

3 $84 \div 7 = 12$

4 $2{,}400 \div 4 = 600$

5 *12-pack:* $\$5.40 \div 12 = \$0.45$ *each. 6-pack:* $\$3.00 \div 6 = \$0.50$ *each.*

6 16 *oz:* $\$4.00 \div 16 = \$0.25/oz$. 28 *oz:* $\$5.60 \div 28 = \$0.20/oz$.

7 $168 \div 5.6 = 30$

8 *Maya:* $54 \div 1.5 = 36$ *pages per hour. Ethan:* $80 \div 2 = 40$ *pages per hour.* $40 > 36$.

Section 1.5

1 4, 20, 10

2 6, 28, 15

3 *Yes*

4 *No*

5 *8 cups of yogurt*

6 *60 students*

7 *6 cups blue, 27 cups white*

Explanations

1 *Row 2:* $\times 2 \to 4$. *Row 3:* $8 \div 2 = 4$, *so* $\times 4 \to 20$. *Row 4:* $\times 5 \to 10$.

2 *Row 2:* $\times 2 \to 6$. *Row 3:* $12 \div 3 = 4$, *so* $\times 4 \to 28$. *Row 4:* $\times 5 \to 15$.

3 *Both simplify to* $2 : 3$. $(6 \div 3 = 2, 9 \div 3 = 3)$ *and* $(14 \div 7 = 2, 21 \div 7 = 3)$.

4 $5 \times 3 = 15$ *but* $8 \times 3 = 24 \neq 20$.

5 $12 \div 3 = 4$. *Yogurt:* $2 \times 4 = 8$.

6 $35 \div 7 = 5$. *Boys:* $5 \times 5 = 25$. *Total:* $25 + 35 = 60$.

7 *Total parts* $= 2 + 9 = 11$. *Each part* $= 33 \div 11 = 3$. *Blue* $= 2 \times 3 = 6$. *White* $= 9 \times 3 = 27$.

> *Section 1.6*

1 $(1, 30)$, $(2, 60)$, $(3, 90)$, $(4, 120)$ | 2 *Yes* | 3 $2 : 5$ | 4 *Line A* | 5 *False*

Explanations

1 *Multiply* 30 *by each hour.* $2 \times 30 = 60$, $3 \times 30 = 90$, $4 \times 30 = 120$.

2 $1 : 3 = 3 : 9$ — *multiply both by* 3.

3 *Look at any point:* $x = 2$, $y = 5$, *so the ratio is* $2 : 5$. *Check:* $4 : 10$ *simplifies to* $2 : 5$ *too.*

4 *Line A rises* 4 *for every* 1, *which is faster than* 3 *for every* 1.

5 *Equivalent ratios always form a straight line through the origin* $(0, 0)$.

> *Section 1.7*

1 $\frac{60}{100} = \frac{3}{5}$; 0.60 | 2 75% | 3 15% | 4 88% | 5 100 *items* | 6 30%

Explanations

1 60% means 60 out of 100. Simplify: $60 \div 20 = 3$, $100 \div 20 = 5$. For the decimal, divide by 100: $60 \div 100 = 0.60$.

2 $\frac{3}{4} = \frac{75}{100}$ because $3 \times 25 = 75$ and $4 \times 25 = 100$. So it is 75%.

3 Multiply the decimal by 100: $0.15 \times 100 = 15$. So $0.15 = 15\%$.

4 88 out of $100 = \frac{88}{100} = 88\%$. When the total is 100, the number correct is the percent.

5 50% of $200 = \frac{50}{100} \times 200 = 100$.

6 $\frac{1}{4} = 25\%$, and $30\% > 25\%$.

> Section 1.8

1 27 | 2 150 | 3 35 | 4 80 | 5 66 | 6 Save \$20; Pay \$60

Explanations

1 Convert: $30\% = 0.30$. Multiply: $0.30 \times 90 = 27$.

2 $75\% = \frac{3}{4}$. Multiply: $\frac{3}{4} \times 200 = 150$. Or use the decimal: $0.75 \times 200 = 150$.

3 10% means one-tenth. Divide by 10: $350 \div 10 = 35$.

4 Set up: $0.25 \times ? = 20$. Divide both sides by 0.25: $20 \div 0.25 = 80$. Check: 25% of $80 = 20$. ✓

5 *Set up:* $0.50\times? = 33$. *Divide:* $33 \div 0.50 = 66$. *Check:* 50% *of* $66 = 33$. ✓

6 25% *of* $\$80 = \$20$. *Pay:* $\$80 - \$20 = \$60$.

> Section 1.9

1 420 *miles* 2 8 *cups red,* 28 *cups white* 3 \$20, \$40, \$60 4 40 *km* 5 15 *bags*

Explanations

1 *Unit rate:* $180 \div 3 = 60$ *mph. In* 7 *hours:* $60 \times 7 = 420$.

2 *Total parts:* 9. *Each part:* $36 \div 9 = 4$. *Red:* $2 \times 4 = 8$. *White:* $7 \times 4 = 28$.

3 *Total parts:* 6. *Each part:* $\$120 \div 6 = \$20$. *Shares:* \$20, \$40, \$60.

4 $8 \times 5 = 40$ *km.*

5 $4 \times 5 = 20$, *so* $3 \times 5 = 15$.

> Section 1.10

1 60 *inches* 2 4 *hours* 3 3,000 *meters* 4 2.5 *kg* 5 2 *hours* 15 *minutes*
6 90 *inches*

Explanations

1. 1 foot $= 12$ inches. Bigger to smaller $\rightarrow$ multiply: $5 \times 12 = 60$.

2. 1 hour $= 60$ minutes. Smaller to bigger $\rightarrow$ divide: $240 \div 60 = 4$.

3. 1 km $= 1{,}000$ m. Bigger to smaller $\rightarrow$ multiply: $3 \times 1{,}000 = 3{,}000$.

4. 1 kg $= 1{,}000$ g. Smaller to bigger $\rightarrow$ divide: $2{,}500 \div 1{,}000 = 2.5$.

5. Divide: $135 \div 60 = 2$ with remainder 15. So 2 full hours and 15 minutes left over.

6. $2.5 \times 36 = 90$.

Chapter 2

Section 2.1

1. 2
2. $\frac{6}{5}$ or $1\frac{1}{5}$
3. $\frac{5}{4}$ or $1\frac{1}{4}$
4. $\frac{2}{3}$
5. 15
6. $\frac{7}{16}$
7. 6 scoops
8. $2\frac{1}{2}$ pieces

1. 4 walls; yes, exactly enough

Explanations

1. $\frac{1}{2} \times \frac{4}{1} = \frac{4}{2} = 2$

2. $\frac{3}{5} \times \frac{2}{1} = \frac{6}{5}$

3 $\frac{5}{6} \times \frac{3}{2} = \frac{15}{12} = \frac{5}{4}$

4 $\frac{4}{9} \times \frac{3}{2} = \frac{12}{18} = \frac{2}{3}$

5 $\frac{3}{1} \times \frac{5}{1} = 15$

6 $\frac{7}{8} \times \frac{1}{2} = \frac{7}{16}$

7 $\frac{3}{4} \div \frac{1}{8} = \frac{3}{4} \times \frac{8}{1} = \frac{24}{4} = 6$

8 $\frac{5}{6} \div \frac{1}{3} = \frac{5}{6} \times \frac{3}{1} = \frac{15}{6} = \frac{5}{2} = 2\frac{1}{2}$

1 $\frac{2}{3} \div \frac{1}{6} = \frac{2}{3} \times \frac{6}{1} = \frac{12}{3} = 4$ *walls. That's exactly* 4*, so yes!*

> Section 2.2

1 63 2 36 3 78 4 52 5 63 *R* 13 6 84 *R* 25 7 10 *buses*
8 204 *cars per hour* 1 206 *R* 15

Explanations

1 $12 \times 63 = 756$

2 $27 \times 36 = 972$

3 $16 \times 78 = 1{,}248$

4 $45 \times 52 = 2{,}340$

5 $14 \times 63 = 882$; $895 - 882 = 13$

6 $38 \times 84 = 3{,}192$; $3{,}217 - 3{,}192 = 25$

7 $342 \div 36 = 9$ *R* 18. *You need* 10 *buses because the remaining* 18 *students still need a bus.*

8 $2{,}856 \div 14 = 204$

1 *A three-digit quotient would mean at least* $23 \times 100 = 2{,}300$ *and up to* $23 \times 999 = 22{,}977$. *Since* 4,753 *is bigger than* 2,300 *but less than* 23,000, *the quotient is a three-digit... wait:* $23 \times 200 = 4{,}600$ *and* $23 \times 210 = 4{,}830 > 4{,}753$. *So quotient is between* 200 *and* 210. *Actually* $23 \times 206 = 4{,}738$, *remainder* 15. *The quotient IS three digits:* 206.

> *Section 2.3*

1 21.719 | 2 36.35 | 3 72.544 | 4 15.937 | 5 25.83 | 6 0.035 | 7 22.8 | 8 13

9 $9.22 | 10 13.2 *seconds* | 1 0.0006

Explanations

5 $63 \times 41 = 2{,}583$; 2 *decimal places*

6 $7 \times 5 = 35$; 3 *decimal places*

7 $91.2 \div 4 = 22.8$

8 $156 \div 12 = 13$

9 $3 \times 2.49 = 7.47$; $7.47 + 1.75 = 9.22$

10 $52.8 \div 4 = 13.2$

1 $12 \times 5 = 60$. *Total decimal places:* $3 + 2 = 5$. *So* 60 *with* 5 *decimal places* $= 0.00060 = 0.0006$.

> *Section 2.4*

1 8 | 2 18 | 3 14 | 4 25 | 5 20 | 6 18 | 7 24 | 8 35 | 9 *6 bags*

10 *24 minutes* | 2 *True* | 4 *False*

Explanations

1 *Factors of* 16: $1, 2, 4, 8, 16$. *Factors of* 40: $1, 2, 4, 5, 8, 10, 20, 40$.

2 $36 = 2^2 \times 3^2$, $54 = 2 \times 3^3$. *Shared:* $2 \times 3^2 = 18$.

3 *Common factors:* $1, 2, 7, 14$. *Greatest is* 14.

4 $100 = 2^2 \times 5^2$, $75 = 3 \times 5^2$. *Shared:* $5^2 = 25$.

5 *Multiples of* 4: $4, 8, 12, 16, 20, \ldots$; *multiples of* 10: $10, 20, \ldots$

6. *Multiples of* 6*:* $6, 12, 18$*; multiples of* 9*:* $9, 18$.

7. $8 = 2^3$, $12 = 2^2 \times 3$. $LCM = 2^3 \times 3 = 24$.

8. 5 *and* 7 *share no common factors, so* $LCM = 5 \times 7 = 35$.

9. $GCF(30, 48) = 6$. *Each bag:* 5 *pencils,* 8 *erasers.*

10. $LCM(12, 8) = 24$.

Section 2.5

1. $4(4+7)$
2. $15(3+2)$
3. $7(3+5)$
4. $18(3+2)$
5. 318
6. $\$96$

Explanations

1. *GCF of* 16 *and* 28 *is* 4. $16 \div 4 = 4$, $28 \div 4 = 7$.

2. *GCF of* 45 *and* 30 *is* 15. $45 \div 15 = 3$, $30 \div 15 = 2$.

3. *GCF of* 21 *and* 35 *is* 7. $21 \div 7 = 3$, $35 \div 7 = 5$.

4. *GCF of* 54 *and* 36 *is* 18. $54 \div 18 = 3$, $36 \div 18 = 2$.

5. $6 \times 53 = 6(50+3) = 300 + 18 = 318$.

6. $12 \times 8 = (10+2) \times 8 = 80 + 16 = 96$.

> Section 2.6

1. -200
2. $+3{,}400$ *or* $3{,}400$
3. $-8°$
4. *No money and no debt*
5. *Less than zero*
6. *False*

Explanations

1. *Below sea level is negative. Sea level is* 0*, so* 200 *feet below is* -200*.*
2. *Above sea level is positive.*
3. *Below zero means negative:* -8*.*
4. *Zero means the account is even — nothing owed and nothing saved.*
5. *Numbers to the left of* 0 *on a number line are always less than* 0*.*
6. $-5 < 3$*. The negative sign matters —* -5 *is to the left of* 3 *on the number line.*

> Section 2.7

1. -9
2. 12
3. 15
4. 8
5. *The diver*
6. *True*

Explanations

1. *Same distance from* 0 *but on the other side.*

2. *Flip the sign:* -12 *becomes* 12.

3. -15 *is* 15 *units from zero.*

4. 8 *is already positive and* 8 *units from zero.*

5. $|-40| = 40$ *and* $|25| = 25$. *The diver is* 40 *units from* 0, *which is farther.*

6. $|-6| = 6$ *and* $|5| = 5$. *Since* $6 > 5$, *the statement is true.*

Section 2.8

1. Between 0 and 1
2. Between -3 and -2
3. Between -2 and -1
4. -3.5
5. $-1, -\frac{1}{2}, \frac{1}{4}, 0.75$
6. True

Explanations

1. $\frac{1}{2} = 0.5$, *which is halfway between* 0 *and* 1, *to the right of* 0.

2. -2.25 *is negative, so left of* 0. *It is* 0.25 *past* -2 *toward* -3.

3. $\frac{5}{3} = 1\frac{2}{3} \approx 1.67$. *So* $-\frac{5}{3}$ *is between* -2 *and* -1.

4. $|-3.5| = 3.5$ *and* $|2.8| = 2.8$. *Since* $3.5 > 2.8$, -3.5 *is farther from* 0.

5. *Convert:* $-1, -0.5, 0.25, 0.75$. *Left to right on the number line.*

6 $-\frac{1}{2} = -0.5$. *They are the same rational number written differently.*

> *Section 2.9*

1 *IV* 2 *II* 3 $(2, 5)$ 4 $(6, 1)$ 5 $(3, -4)$ 6 *True*

Explanations

1 *x is positive, y is negative $\rightarrow$ Quadrant IV.*

2 *x is negative, y is positive $\rightarrow$ Quadrant II.*

3 *Flip the y-coordinate: -5 becomes 5. The x stays the same.*

4 *Flip the x-coordinate: -6 becomes 6. The y stays the same.*

5 *First reflection: $(-3, -4)$. Second reflection: $(3, -4)$. Both signs flipped.*

6 *When $x = 0$, the point is on the y-axis, no matter what y is.*

> *Section 2.10*

1 $<$ 2 $>$ 3 $=$ 4 $>$ 5 $-8, -1, 0, 3, 5$ 6 *Tuesday*

Explanations

1 -7 is farther left on the number line, so $-7 < -3$.

2 0 is to the right of every negative number.

3 They are the same number.

4 Any positive number is greater than any negative number.

5 Place on a number line: leftmost is least, rightmost is greatest.

6 $-9 < -4$, so Tuesday was colder. Farther below zero means colder.

Section 2.11

1 7 | 2 8 | 3 10 | 4 8 | 5 8 *blocks* | 6 12 *units*

Explanations

1 Same x. $|4 - (-3)| = |4 + 3| = 7$ units.

2 Same y. $|-5 - 3| = |-8| = 8$ units.

3 Same $x = 0$. $|-6 - 4| = |-10| = 10$ units.

4 Same x. $|-1 - (-9)| = |-1 + 9| = 8$ units.

5 Same x. $|5 - (-3)| = |8| = 8$ blocks.

6 Same y. $|-7-5| = |-12| = 12$ units.

Chapter 3

Section 3.1

1 7^3 2 2^5 3 64 4 70 5 20 6 Jake

Explanations

1 The base 7 is multiplied 3 times.

2 The base 2 is multiplied 5 times.

3 $4 \times 4 = 16$, then $16 \times 4 = 64$.

4 Exponent: $10^2 = 100$. Multiply: $6 \times 5 = 30$. Subtract: $100 - 30 = 70$.

5 Parentheses: $8 + 2 = 10$. Exponent: $10^2 = 100$. Divide: $100 \div 5 = 20$.

6 Multiply first: $4 \times 2 = 8$. Then add: $3 + 8 = 11$. Maria added before multiplying.

Section 3.2

1 $8 + k$ 2 $m - 4$ 3 $3w + 10$ 4 $p \div 6$ 6 B 7 False

Explanations

1 "Sum" means addition: $8 + k$.

2 "Less than" means subtract from m: $m - 4$.

3 "Triple" means $3 \times w = 3w$. Then add 10.

4 "Divided by" puts p on top: $p \div 6$.

6 "Twice x" is $2x$. "9 more" means add 9: $9 + 2x$.

7 $10 \div n \neq n \div 10$. Order matters in division.

> Section 3.3

1 3 | 2 1 | 3 8 | 4 5 and $(x + 3)$ | 5 True | 6 False

Explanations

1 The terms are $7m$, $3n$, and 5.

2 y means $1 \cdot y$, so the coefficient is 1.

3 8 is the only term without a variable.

4 5 is multiplied by the group $(x + 3)$.

5 $9x$ *means* $9 \times x$, *so* 9 *and* x *are factors.*

6 4 *is a constant, but* $2y$ *is a variable term, not a constant.*

Section 3.4

1 27 2 29 3 10 4 15 5 34 *cm* 6 \$35

Explanations

1 $5(6) - 3 = 30 - 3 = 27.$

2 $5^2 + 4 = 25 + 4 = 29.$

3 $(8 + 12) \div 2 = 20 \div 2 = 10.$

4 $3(9 - 4) = 3(5) = 15.$

5 $2(12) + 2(5) = 24 + 10 = 34$ *cm.*

6 $20 + 0.10(150) = 20 + 15 = 35$ *dollars.*

Section 3.5

1 $8x - 4$ 2 $2y + 18$ 3 $11m + 3$ 4 *Yes* 5 *False* 6 $8a + 7$

Explanations

1. Combine like terms: $6x + 2x = 8x$.
2. Distribute: $2 \times y + 2 \times 9$.
3. Distribute: $6m + 3 + 5m$. Combine: $11m + 3$.
4. $4(3 + 2) = 4(5) = 20$. $4(3) + 8 = 12 + 8 = 20$. Same result.
5. $3x + 5x = 8x$, not $8x^2$. You add coefficients, not multiply the variable.
6. Combine: $10a - 2a = 8a$. The constant stays.

Section 3.6

1. $25 + 10m$
2. $50 + nw$
3. $3l$
4. Let f = number of friends. Each pays $14 \div f$ dollars.
5. False

Explanations

1. Fixed fee: 25. Monthly cost: $10m$. Total: $25 + 10m$.
2. Start with 50, add n songs for w weeks: $50 + nw$.
3. Area $=$ length $\times$ width $= l \times 3 = 3l$.
4. The unknown is how many friends share, so use f.

5 s is the side length. It can be any positive number — the formula works for every square.

Section 3.7

1 $y = 11$

2 $m = 22$

3 $k = 9$

4 $n = 40$

5 $m + 7 = 19$, so $m = 12$

6 $\frac{b}{3} = 14$, so $b = 42$

Explanations

1 Subtract 9: $y = 20 - 9 = 11$.

2 Add 7: $m = 15 + 7 = 22$.

3 Divide by 6: $k = 54 \div 6 = 9$.

4 Multiply by 5: $n = 8 \times 5 = 40$.

5 Subtract 7: $m = 19 - 7 = 12$. The magazine costs $\$12$.

6 Multiply by 3: $b = 14 \times 3 = 42$.

Section 3.8

1 $a < 13$

2 $w \leq 50$

3 $d \geq 20$

4 $t < 0$

5 No

6 False

Explanations

1 "Under 13" means less than 13: $a < 13$.

2 "At most 50" means 50 or less: $w \leq 50$.

3 "At least 20" means 20 or more: $d \geq 20$.

4 "Below 0" means less than 0: $t < 0$.

5 $5 > 5$ is false. 5 is not greater than itself. It would be a solution to $x \geq 5$.

6 $n \leq 10$ has infinitely many solutions: $10, 9.5, 0, -3, \ldots$ any number that is 10 or less.

Section 3.9

1 Closed circle at 2, shade right

2 Open circle at 7, shade left

3 Yes

4 No

5 $t > 75$; open circle at 75, shade right

6 $x \leq -3$

Explanations

1 $\geq$ includes 2 (closed) and means greater (right).

2 $<$ does not include 7 (open) and means less (left).

3 $4 \leq 4$ is true because 4 equals 4, and $\leq$ includes equality.

4 $-1 > 0$ is false. -1 is to the left of 0.

5 "More than 75" means > 75. Not equal, so open circle.

6 Closed circle means $\leq$ or $\geq$. Shading left means less than: $x \leq -3$.

> Section 3.10

1 Independent: hours (t); Dependent: distance (d)

2 Independent: hours (h); Dependent: battery left (b

3 $c = 10p$; cost is \$70

4 15

5 False

Explanations

1 You choose how long to drive. Distance depends on time: $d = 60t$.

2 Battery depends on how many hours have passed.

3 $c = 10(7) = 70$ dollars.

4 $d = 3(5) = 15$.

5 x is independent (you choose it). y depends on x.

Chapter 4

> Section 4.1

1 20 in^2	2 54 cm^2	3 7 m^2	4 18 ft^2	5 12 m^2	6 True

Explanations

1 $\frac{1}{2} \times 8 \times 5 = 20.$

2 $\frac{1}{2} \times 12 \times 9 = 54.$

3 $\frac{1}{2} \times 3.5 \times 4 = 7.$

4 $\frac{1}{2} \times 6 \times 6 = 18.$

5 $\frac{1}{2} \times 4 \times 6 = 12$ m^2 *of fabric.*

6 *Both give* $\frac{1}{2} \times 10 \times 4 = 20$ *and* $\frac{1}{2} \times 8 \times 5 = 20.$

Section 4.2

1 21 m^2	2 55 ft^2	3 30 cm^2	4 24 in^2	5 1,500 m^2	6 True

Explanations

1 $A = 7 \times 3 = 21.$

2 $A = 10 \times 5.5 = 55.$

3 $\frac{1}{2}(4+8)(5) = \frac{1}{2}(60) = 30.$

4 $\frac{1}{2}(3+9)(4) = \frac{1}{2}(48) = 24.$

5 $\frac{1}{2}(40+60)(30) = \frac{1}{2}(3000) = 1500.$

6 *Both use* $A = b \times h = 24.$ *Same formula, same area.*

> Section 4.3

1 120 cm^3 | 2 48 in^3 | 3 12 m^3 | 4 $\frac{1}{8}$ ft^3 | 5 2,400 in^3 | 6 3 *cm*

Explanations

1 $6 \times 4 \times 5 = 120.$

2 $8 \times 3 \times 2 = 48.$

3 $1.5 \times 2 = 3.$ *Then* $3 \times 4 = 12.$

4 $\frac{1}{2} \times \frac{1}{2} \times \frac{1}{2} = \frac{1}{8}.$

5 $20 \times 10 \times 12 = 2400.$

6 *Base area:* $5 \times 4 = 20.$ *Height:* $60 \div 20 = 3$ *cm.*

> Section 4.4

1 6 *units* | 2 8 *units* | 3 6 *units* | 4 4 *units* | 5 36 *units*

Explanations

1. $|4-(-2)| = |6| = 6.$

2. $|3-(-5)| = |8| = 8.$

3. $|6-0| = 6.$ *The base runs from* $(0,0)$ *to* $(6,0).$

4. $|2-(-2)| = 4.$ *Each side is* 4 *units long.*

5. *Length:* $|6-(-4)| = 10.$ *Width:* $|5-(-3)| = 8.$ *Perimeter:* $2(10)+2(8) = 36.$

Section 4.5

1. 15 *sq units*
2. 36 *sq units*
3. 24 *sq units*
4. 12 *sq units*
5. 21 *sq units*

Explanations

1. $5 \times 3 = 15.$

2. *Length:* $|3-(-3)| = 6.$ *Width:* $|4-(-2)| = 6.$ *Area:* $6 \times 6 = 36.$

3. *Base* $= 8,$ *height* $= 6.$ *Area* $= \frac{1}{2} \times 8 \times 6 = 24.$

4. *Base* $= |5-1| = 4.$ *Height* $= |7-1| = 6.$ *Area* $= \frac{1}{2} \times 4 \times 6 = 12.$

5. *Bottom rectangle:* $6 \times 2 = 12.$ *Top-left rectangle:* $3 \times 3 = 9.$ *Total:* $12 + 9 = 21.$

> Section 4.6

1. 88 in^2
2. 150 cm^2
3. 242 m^2
4. 52 ft^2
5. 132 cm^2

Explanations

1. $2(6)(4) + 2(6)(2) + 2(4)(2) = 48 + 24 + 16 = 88.$
2. *A cube has 6 equal faces:* $6 \times 5^2 = 6 \times 25 = 150.$
3. $2(10)(3) + 2(10)(7) + 2(3)(7) = 60 + 140 + 42 = 242.$
4. $2(2)(3) + 2(2)(4) + 2(3)(4) = 12 + 16 + 24 = 52.$
5. *2 triangles:* $2 \times \frac{1}{2}(3)(4) = 12.$ *3 rectangles:* $3(10) + 4(10) + 5(10) = 120.$ *Total:* $12 + 120 = 132.$

Chapter 5

> Section 5.1

1. Not statistical
2. Statistical
3. Statistical
4. Not statistical
5. Answers vary

Explanations

1. *There is only one answer (Paris). It does not vary.*

2 *Different students have different numbers of pets. The answers vary.*

3 *Heights vary from student to student.*

4 *There is only one answer (56). It does not vary.*

5 *Any question whose answers change from person to person. Example: "How many minutes do you spend on homework?" Different students spend different amounts of time.*

Section 5.2

1 Bunched together

2 Yes, 25

3 Around 23–24

4 Student B

Explanations

1 *The values only range from 10 to 14 (range = 4). They are close to each other.*

2 *Most values are between 3 and 8. The value 25 is far from the rest.*

3 *Most values cluster near these numbers. The data is symmetric around the middle.*

4 *Student A's range is $13 - 10 = 3$. Student B's range is $30 - 2 = 28$. Student B's data is much more spread out.*

Section 5.3

1 Mean $= 7$, Median $= 7$

2 Mean $= 16.25$, Median $= 16.5$

3 Mean $= 22.8$; not a good description

4 Mean drops from 87 to 79.2

Explanations

1 *Mean:* $(3 + 5 + 7 + 9 + 11) \div 5 = 35 \div 5 = 7$. *Median: middle value is* 7.

2 *Mean:* $(12 + 15 + 18 + 20) \div 4 = 65 \div 4 = 16.25$. *Median:* $(15 + 18) \div 2 = 16.5$.

3 $(2 + 3 + 4 + 5 + 100) \div 5 = 22.8$. *Most values are around* 2–5. *The outlier* 100 *pulls the mean way up. The median* (4) *is more typical.*

4 *Original mean:* $435 \div 5 = 87$. *New mean:* $475 \div 6 \approx 79.2$. *The low score pulled the mean down.*

Section 5.4

1 16 | 2 $Q1 = 5$, $Q3 = 12$, $IQR = 7$ | 3 2.4 | 4 0 | 5 *Team A*

Explanations

1 $26 - 10 = 16$.

2 *Lower half:* $3, 5, 7 \rightarrow Q1 = 5$. *Upper half:* $10, 12, 14 \rightarrow Q3 = 12$. *IQR:* $12 - 5 = 7$.

3 *Distances from* 8: $4, 2, 0, 2, 4$. *MAD:* $(4 + 2 + 0 + 2 + 4) \div 5 = 12 \div 5 = 2.4$.

4 *Every value equals the mean* (10). *All distances are* 0. $MAD = 0$.

5 Team A range: $70 - 50 = 20$. Team B range: $100 - 20 = 80$. Team A's scores are much closer together, so they are more consistent.

> Section 5.5

1 10 days | 2 72°F | 3 19 students | 4 60–69 | 5 Histogram

Explanations

1 $1 + 3 + 4 + 2 = 10$.

2 72°F has 4 dots, more than any other value.

3 $12 + 7 = 19$ students scored in the 80–89 or 90–100 bins.

4 Only 3 students scored in the 60–69 bin.

5 With 500 data points, a dot plot would be too crowded. A histogram groups the ages into intervals, making the display easier to read.

> Section 5.6

1 $5, 8, 15, 24, 28$ | 2 Median $= 7$, IQR $= 6$ | 3 50% | 4 25 | 5 Class A

Explanations

1 Min $= 5$. $Q1$: median of $5, 8, 12 = 8$. Median $= 15$. $Q3$: median of $20, 24, 28 = 24$. Max $= 28$.

2 Median: $(6+8) \div 2 = 7$. Q1: median of $2, 4, 6 = 4$. Q3: median of $8, 10, 12 = 10$. IQR: $10 - 4 = 6$.

3 The box (Q1 to Q3) always contains the middle 50% of the data.

4 $Q3 - Q1 = 80 - 55 = 25$.

5 Class A's IQR is only 10, meaning the middle 50% of scores are within 10 points. Class B's middle 50% spans 30 points—much more spread out.

Section 5.7

1 Mean = 20, range = 10

2 Median

3 Class A

4 Store A is more consistent

5 Not necessarily

Explanations

1 Mean: $100 \div 5 = 20$. Range: $25 - 15 = 10$. Sample summary: "The typical value is 20, and the data spans 10 units."

2 The outlier 50 pulls the mean up to 11.5, but most values are around 6. The median (6) better represents a typical value.

3 Class A has a higher median ($85 > 80$) and a smaller IQR ($8 < 20$), meaning scores were higher and more consistent.

4 Both average \$400 per day, but Store A's sales vary by about \$50 from the mean, while Store B's vary by \$150. Store A has steadier sales.

5 The teams use different scales. The soccer team's range is 3 out of a mean of about 2.6 (over 100% of the mean). The basketball team's range is 30 out of a mean of 75 (about 40%). Comparing ranges only makes sense when the data is on the same scale.

Great Job! Keep Learning with ViewMath!

*Keep up the great work! Visit **viewmath.com/MA-Grade6** for free lessons, practice, and more.*

Study Guide

Scan Me

Step-by-Step

Scan Me

3 Practice Tests

Scan Me

5 Practice Tests

Scan Me

7 Practice Tests

Scan Me

10 Practice Tests

Scan Me

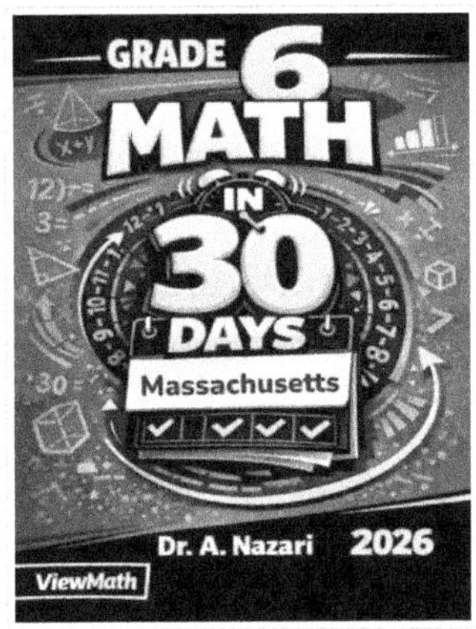

Math in 30 Days

Scan Me

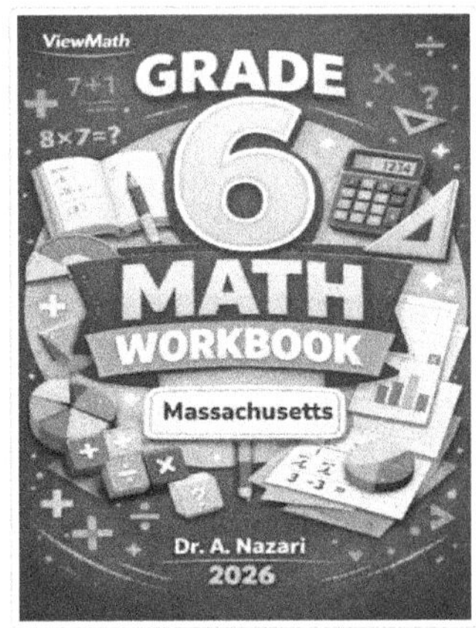

Quizzes

Scan Me

uthor's Final Note

hope you enjoyed this book as much as I enjoyed writing it. Whether you are a student working through the material, parent supporting your child's learning, or a teacher guiding your class, I have tried to make this book as clear and ngaging as possible. I hope I have succeeded. If you have any suggestions for improvement, please let me know. I ould love to hear from you.

he accuracy of calculations is very important to me. We have done our best, but I also expect that I have made some inor errors. Constant improvement is the name of the game. If you find any errors, please let me know. I will fix them the next edition.

***or students:** Your learning journey does not end here. I have written a series of books to help you learn math. Make ire you browse through them. I especially recommend workbooks and practice tests to help you prepare for your xams.*

***or parents:** Thank you for investing in your child's education. I encourage you to explore the companion resources vailable online to help support your child outside the classroom.*

***or teachers:** Thank you for the invaluable work you do every day. I hope this book serves as a useful resource in your assroom. Feel free to reach out if you have suggestions or would like to discuss how best to use this book with your udents.*

also enjoy reading your reviews. If you have a moment, please leave a review on where you found this book. It will help hers find this book. If you have any questions or comments, please feel free to contact me at nazari@ViewMath.com.

nd one last thing: Remember to use online resources for additional help. I recommend using the resources on `https:` `/ViewMath.com` You can find video lessons, practice problems, and more. You can also use the online companion for is book to track your progress and access additional resources.

ishing all students the best in their studies, parents every success in supporting their children, and teachers continued spiration in their classrooms!

. A. Nazari

www.ingramcontent.com/pod-product-compliance
Lightning Source LLC
LaVergne TN
LVHW080049210926
848481LV00011B/3313
* 9 7 9 8 8 9 5 9 9 8 6 7 0 *